DE/TACHED

PARTHIAN

"Attachment is the great fabricator of illusion; reality can be attained only by someone who is detached."

— Simone Weil

DE/TACHED

PARTHIAN

Parthian
The Old Surgery
Napier Street
Cardigan
SA43 1ED
www.parthianbooks.co.uk

Published with the financial support of the Welsh Books Council.

First published in 2006
© The Authors

Foreword © Menna Elfyn
All Rights Reserved

ISBN 1 902638 97 2
    9 781902 638973

Cover art courtesy of Mike Smith

Printed and bound by Dinefwr Press, Llandybïe, Wales
Typeset by logodædaly

British Library Cataloguing in Publication Data

A cataloguing record for this book is available from the British
Library.

Contents

The attentive reader will notice variations in spellings in this book. Where US English was used in the original it has been retained. Otherwise British English spelling is employed.

A special thanks to the De/tached committee:

Nicky Herriot, Chair

Kelly Fitzgerald, Co-editor

Sandra Mackness, Co-editor

Ansley Moon, Publishing Liaison

Foreword

In the writing world, attachment takes on a new meaning. It is no longer an abstraction but a real, solid entity, one that often arrives at the speed of light through email. One minute one is detached, writing alone at one's desk and the next minute an 'attachment' arrives with the similar sense of urgency as when it was sent. One needs to open it, and through opening, one bares one's soul and puts it under the spotlight. And suddenly detachment and attachment come together briefly, through the act of reading. Alone. But the true writer, whose work is always to 'connect', as Forster suggested, is also aware of that other sense of de/tachment, that comes with editing one's work. That takes on a new order as the creator gains the necessary distance from which to view things anew. That sense of alienation and necessity is what Adrienne Rich wrote about in trying to explain the whole process of writing.

While this book arrived through a series of attachments, therefore, its theme is necessarily one of de/tachment. The inspiration for the title came from an observation made by Simone Weil, one of the greatest thinkers and activists of the 20th century, who wrote:

'attachment is the great fabricator of illusion: reality can be attained only by someone who is detached.'

After reading the Upanishads and the whole notion of Atman, which she saw as mirroring Plato's idea of the good, she believed the human soul should attempt to identify itself to the point of self-extinction. In her view, the individual faced the fundamental problem of the duality of attachment and renunciation.

Weil also said that 'by the power of words, we always mean their power of illusion…'. In this collection we are undoubtedly confronted with the notion that illusion and disillusion are part of the human condition. There is a blend of writing here, primarily concerned with the absence of connection, or a sense of disengagement.

The works of Nadine Fry, Caroline Hawkes and Ansley Moon are suffused with the sense of loss and longing; sensual and stark images magnify the fragility of life as we identify the heartache of the vulnerable. Bethany Pope too, straddles the forces of good and evil in her chilling Gothic tales which challenge our conception of the human condition,

Judith Barrow and Sue Moss weave dramatic silences within speech as they vividly enact the fragmentation of relationships. Sharon Tregenza deals deftly with geographical distances as well as hidden desires, while Sandra Mackness's story gleams with the beauty of love's brittle fragments.

Jacqui Burns entertains us with a counterpoise between belonging as opposed to freedom, as does David Jones's carefully-crafted song, reminiscing of faraway days with musical echoes. Inventiveness is the key in Nicky Herriot's work, as the reader takes us into the realm of simulation and the fear of the undesired. Dian Jenkins's work in the Welsh language is also testimony to the resonance of telling a new tale in an old tongue.

Kelly Fitzgerald's journalistic vigour is a delight to read as we enter the life of an artist, Mike Smith, whose work captures the 'zeitgeist 'of this book. We learn of his artistic journey and his way of life through art. His telling comment, 'I'm in the company of artists, which has allowed me to become more experimental,' is hopefully a vision the writers of this volume share.

This is the ninth year of the M.A. Creative Writing programme. Every year generates its own enthusiasm and momentum in publishing an anthology. That important sense of ownership this year too, from inception to fruition, is solely the work of a small editorial team who have worked with joie de vivre. In that respect, the title belies the whole notion of detachment! They are also grateful for the support of Dr Paul Wright, Head of Creative Arts and Humanities, and support of Faculty of Arts and Social Sciences, especially Head of faculty, Kevin Matherick, and also to the college for their financial commitment and support towards this venture.

Many writers have attested to the instrumental enrichment of a good book. As Maxim Gorky once said: 'It is to books that I owe everything that is good in me'. This splendid fusion of writing about everyday relationships and desire, longing, loss, pain, and the uncertainty of our destinies, reminds us all of what it is to be human, possessing our 'need for roots' and at times 'de/tachment'. For as we hold our breath now and again in life, we oscillate, daily, between giving and receiving, and in doing so, strive for the equilibrium of another of Weil's aspirations, towards 'gravity and grace'.

Menna Elfyn
Trinity College, Carmarthen.

DE/TACHED

Ride Home

Bethany Pope

The jeepney rolled through the dusty barrio outside of Manila, sending plumes of dirt up toward the sky to fall, moistened by the humid atmosphere, patting back to earth like rain. It was large and filthy, brightly coloured with paint and decorations and exhaling fluorocarbons in a black cloud that filled the air behind it. This one was a converted flatbed truck. The sides were shorn off and replaced with plywood walls and benches. It was roofed, shanty-style, with aluminium siding, and un-glassed windows were cut into the walls.

The driver sat in the front of the cab, slowing down for passengers every two hundred yards or so. He would slow down, but never stop. The potential patrons would walk quickly to keep up, hand their money to the strong boy by the door, and then grab hold of the metal rail attached to the wall, or his hand. Hopefully, either way they would be pulled on, although I once saw an old man who couldn't keep up. He handed up his money, caught hold of the rail, and ran a few stuttering steps by the side of the road before finally stumbling, his grip slipping. He fell into the dust, badly startling some scrawny, mottled chickens that were questing for worms in the gutter by his head.

Today there had been no accidents, although I secretly longed for one to break the monotony of the ride. I was travelling with my mother then. She could still travel, when I was very young, before the disease raged through her body, constraining her to her bed. We were on our way back from her weekly visit to the Sisters, a group of nuns who ran an orphanage a short distance outside of the Subic Bay Naval Base. She would talk, sometimes whispered mouthings, about concern over the revolution and the guerrillas that roamed, secret in the forests. She would help with minor chores, bring them packaged, rationed food that she secreted from the company store, and occasionally money, when she could get it.

I went with her occasionally. I would play with the children, most of whom were about my age. Their heads were large for their bodies, their bellies distended with starvation and worms, their arms and legs hung limp like straw, and just as brittle. And yet, we played. They knew few English words, and my Tagalog was rudimentary at best, but when you're six years old, you can work around language barriers. So we ran in a herd, rolling and tackling, and sometimes sliding in the rich, black dust.

After my mother's visit, after the sweat had collected on my forehead and plastered the dirt to my skin, after she clucked with marginal disappointment at the large rip in my bright yellow dress, we caught the jeepney and headed for home.

4

We were sitting on a plywood bench between a fish merchant still holding two large and stinking examples of his ware, inexplicably wrapped in page three of an errant British newspaper, and a housewife in a faded but still brightly coloured dress. She would occasionally speak to my mother, commenting on the heat, praying for rain, remarking on the lightness of my fine light-strawberry hair and the paleness of my skin. She ran her fingers through it, through the sweat-drenched clumps of hair and my sticky, filthy skin.

"Kayo may isa anak na babae maganda," she smiled and gently smoothed down a wrinkle in my bright and filthy dress.

"Salamat," my mother said, pleased.

I placed my head in her lap, smelling the strange mixture of vanilla Jean'tu perfume, the clinging remnants of this morning's Dove soap, and the hot-wet smell of her soured sweat. I watched droplets of my own sweat collect on my bangs and fall with a pop onto the wooden floor, changing the colour of the dirt it touched.

The jeepney rolled almost to a stop to pass some caribou that had broken free from their bamboo enclosure. The boy that was herding them shouted and waved with the stick in his hand. His body was dark and glistening with sweat. He was naked from the waist up, clad only in off-white pantaloons and rice-woven shoes.

The air was hot and still, pregnant with the summer storms still a month away. The sky was bright and streaked with the grey contrails from planes that landed and left from Clark.

Gunshots broke the stillness of the air, rattling like backfiring cars, too close together. My mother's hands clamped down on my skull and her nails clenched in, drawing blood and sending a few torn loose hairs drifting to the floor.

For the first time in my experience, the jeepney stopped.

I tried to raise my head, but her fingers held me down. I could hear her blood pulsing in her stomach, the very beating of her heart. I felt something warmer than the air strike me in a wave down my arm. My dress was splashed with blood that fell like long denied rain around me and into the creases in the floor. My mother ducked down, pulling me into the dirt, pulling me into the worn-in oils of the plywood bench, pulling splinters into my skin.

The housewife beside me slid, breathless, to the floor.

Her shoulder exploded in a fountain of red. Her hair fell in a torrent around her face and her screams raged like water through the air.

I watched her sink into the dirt on the floor. I watched the brown turn maroon with her spreading blood. I watched her crying, her tears collecting in the furrows and the cracks, her breath blowing over, stirring the dust. I watched her convulse and foam. The fish merchant dropped his stinking, rotting catch, fresh this morning, and dove down beside her. He tore off his belt and tried to cinch the wound shut, trying to tie it off over the place where her shoulder should have been.

I watched him struggle; I watched her still. I heard the ticking of the engine and the patting of her blood, the gasps of my mother and the current of the blood that flowed inside of her. I closed my eyes against her dress and drank her scent like water, and eventually, I slept.

I was very young.

I slept through the ride back to the base, slept through the transfer from the gunmetal-green Humvee to the waiting circle of my father's arms. I slept calmly and peacefully through the night.

Much later I connected the pieces and understood my mother's fear. I understood the cries of "Gringo" that echoed with the gunfire. I understood the dangers of a pregnant storm. For now, for then, I slept like the earth after the rain. I grew and drank life like living water. I lived.

Mills and Boon

Sharon Tregenza

In my shop queue a lady was reading
A romance by Mills and Boon.
"You go on ahead,"
she excitedly said.
"He's just carried her into his room."

Stray

Sue Moss

She shoved her hands deep into the pockets of her cord jacket, balled them into tight fists and straightaway wished she'd worn her good coat. She scuffed a stone to the gutter. She knew he'd be late. He was always late.

Picking through the contents of her handbag till her fingers fell on the cellophane packet, she pulled out a cigarette. Lighting it was a trial in the steady wind. She sucked deeply, drawing cold air along with the smoke. The effect was calming; it had a rhythm and purpose. She loved to smoke and was good at it. She dragged it right down to the butt, the very last ember, then flicked the thing into the street where it lay glowing bravely till it died.

Suddenly, he arrived, pulling up fast in a car she didn't recognise, spraying her jeans with rainwater. He stretched across the front seat, yanked open the door, looked up at her and smiled. She glared a response.

"Come on girl, get in, it's freezing."

"Like I don't know."

"Sling your bag in the back and hurry up. It's freezing."

She dropped the bag in the back seat, took her cigarettes and purse, held them in her lap, settled herself in the passenger side and stared ahead. He tried to make eye contact.

"Right, we're off."

"You're late."

"Not very."

"You're late. I've stood here twenty minutes at least."

"I needed petrol, don't wanna stop."

"You said ten o'clock."

"I'm here now."

She stared at the road in front. He shifted gear, pulled into traffic.

"You took your time though. You've got everything, have you?"

"Jen, for God's sake. I'm here now. I've apologised already."

She glared at him. "You have not said sorry."

"I did."

"You did not. You never do. You did not say sorry to me for keeping me stood there for twenty bloody minutes. I'm freezing cold. You did not say sorry!" She fiddled with the pack of cigarettes.

He pushed into fifth, moved easily into the exit lane, hurled abuse at an overtaking lorry and pulled onto the motorway. He stared at the road ahead.

"Can you turn the heating up?"

"What heating?"

"Are you serious? It's bloody January? Why get a car with no heater? My God, Sonny, this is so typical!"

10

She slunk into her seat, forced her fists deeper into her pockets and glared out the side window. "I won't even ask about the radio." They drove in silence for four miles.

"Where'd you get it anyway?"

"Get what?"

"The car. Where'd you get this bloody freezing car?"

"Tony. He got it from a friend."

"When?"

"What?"

"When'd he get it?"

"Christ, Jen, who cares? Tony got the car. I'm driving the car. It's what you wanted. I picked you up, like you wanted. At the exact spot, like you said. We're on the motorway, on the first of January. We're going, like we planned. Everything you bloody wanted – it's done. So shut up moaning."

"I'm bloody freezing!"

"Well, you wanted January, honey."

"I'm just saying …"

"Yeah, well you can stop saying." For a second, their eyes met. Her face crumpled like a spoiled kid's. He saw the smudge of lipstick on her mouth. He turned his attention to the road; she touched his arm.

"Don't shout at me, Sonny. You know I hate it when you shout at me."

"Okay, well stop going on."

"Can we stop soon?"

"No way. I wanna get there."

"Sonny, I'm cold, let's stop for coffee soon."

"The next stop is six miles, okay, maybe then."

11

*   *   *

He drove until dusk, as against all odds she'd fallen asleep. Out of boredom, he guessed. She stirred as he tugged the handbrake.

"Where are we?"

"South."

"What happened?" She stretched, "Is it night? Where are we? Are we there yet?"

"No." He splayed his fingers on the wheel. They ached and he hadn't thought to bring gloves. He cracked his knuckles, one by one they popped, and he repeated it until she cried, "Sonny, I hate that – stop, okay."

"I'm hungry. Thought we'd stop for a bit, grab a coffee or something stronger." She stretched again, yawned loudly, her mouth wide open.

"Good, then let's eat."

They ordered burgers and coffee for him, brandy for her.

"How long was I asleep?"

"Since Birmingham."

"How long?"

"It doesn't matter, Jen, you didn't miss anything."

"Did I snore?"

He laughed, "Man, like nothing on earth." She leaned across the table, punched him hard on the arm. He acted up, "Ooh…aah, get off – mad woman on the loose…ooh." She was on him at once, hissing, "Shut up, shut up, don't draw attention to us."

He sighed. "No one cares, Jen. Look at us. We couldn't be more boring." He drained his cup, held it at his lips, and watched her sip her brandy. There was nothing boring about her. The first time he saw her he couldn't turn away. Her long lashes framed wide-open,

12

deep brown eyes. That night she'd worn this same cord jacket, and the long black jeans chosen to show her figure. Not thin, not heavy. Tony dragged him to a party where he picked out this wide-eyed girl clinging to the edge of the group. When he asked her to dance she grinned but stayed in her seat clutching a glass. He'd given up then, but returned later to find her in the same seat, as though she'd not moved – like she'd been waiting for him all along.

He'd reached to take her hand and noticed something. It was fleeting, a flinch, but he'd noticed. They'd moved to the dance floor. He watched her sway beneath the flashing lights, her eyes gypsy-black. She bent her head away from him. When she returned his gaze she hesitated, looked at the floor, the ceiling, anywhere but him.

*   *   *

"We off then?"

"Uh huh."

"Jesus, it's even colder than before." She pulled her jacket tight. "Do you think we'll get there tonight?"

"Dunno. We could stop overnight."

"It's New Year's Day, Sonny, where're we gonna stay?"

"I'll keep going then. Like you wanted. Non-stop – keep going till we get there."

"I'm just cold. Haven't you got a blanket in this useless car?"

"You're lucky we've got the car."

"How much did he charge you?"

"Five hundred."

"You're the end."

13

*　　*　　*

They drove on; she fell asleep again. When he slowed to change lanes she woke suddenly, her eyes bright with fear. She struggled to speak, then said, "I was thinking of nothing at all, then I was thinking of everything in the world. What'd you think that means?"

"Dunno." The traffic was heavy and the weather worsening by the minute. He worried there'd be snow. She shook her head and sat up.

"Well you could give it a little thought."

"I'm driving, Jen. I'm tired too. We want to keep going, don't we? Like you said, we'll keep on. I'm not up for conversation right now, okay. I'm sorry."

"HA!" She shrieked, punching the air with her fist. "Ha! At last."

"What the hell?"

"You said it!"

"Said what?"

"At bloody last. You said it."

"Christ."

"I knew you'd say it! I just knew it. I said to myself 'He'll say it, he'll say it if it's the last thing he says to me.'"

"You are bloody nuts. Said what?"

"Sorry!"

"Huh?"

"Ha. You said sorry, Sonny. You said sorry!"

"I'm pulling over." He shook his head, trying to clear it.

She shrieked again, "Naaah…keep driving." She taunted him, "Sonny said sorry, Sonny said sorry."

14

"I'm telling you lady, I ain't going any further till I know what this is about."

She was buoyant now, the cold a thing forgotten. She dipped in her bag, pulled out a cigarette. His breath fogged the windscreen.

"No! Wait till we stop."

"I wanna smoke now!"

"Shut up." His hand flew from the wheel. She recoiled, sunk back in her seat.

"What, Sonny, what you gonna do? Hit me?"

"No, I'm just trying to drive."

"All right, I know! I want a cigarette though."

*   *   *

Two miles on, they pulled into the car park of a motel: rooms at forty-nine pounds per night, a special New Year's offer. There were vacancies. She climbed from the car, hauled her bag after her. They checked in together, paying with cash, and then crossed the car park to find their room.

"Where are your things?"

He shrugged, "What things?"

"Your stuff. Have you even brought a bag, an overnight one, where's your stuff?"

He shook his head, "I've brought nothing. I thought that was the point. No baggage you said, just us, nothing else."

"I know, but you'll need a change of clothes, at least a shirt. Some overnight stuff."

"I didn't think we'd be overnight. I've got cash. I can buy anything I need when we get there."

"Well, what about now, what about tonight? You never think, do you? It's all the time down to me to get everything organised. Even then you can't meet me on time."

"I didn't plan to stay anywhere tonight, did I – this wasn't part of the great plan, was it?"

She threw her bag to the floor. "Don't start that. Don't you start that with me now. If you'd got us a half decent car we could've kept driving. But no, as bloody usual you get your useless brother to get us a heap of shit and now we're stuck. Don't you all the time try blaming me!"

He walked away from her, stuck the key in the door, turned it and walked in.

"Hey, enough swearing, I've got cash, okay. We'll be there tomorrow."

"Well we'd better be." She dived into her makeup bag. She pulled out a toothbrush, then another. She threw it at him. "You can have this, I brought two."

She began hanging her clothes in the tiny wardrobe, then pulled on a cotton nightshirt and flicked her cigarette butt into the toilet, pulling the chain.

He sat on the edge of the double bed, flicked on the TV. She was at him in a flash. "No way. I'm exhausted. Get washed, then we can get to bed and make an early start tomorrow. I want to get there, Sonny." She jabbed her finger at his chest. "You better make up for this."

The heater in the room read twenty-seven degrees. He moved to adjust it. She leapt at him. "You must be fucking joking. You leave that. I've been freezing my arse off in that fucking wreck of a car the whole bastard day, so you just leave it on hot, buster. Okay."

She climbed into the bed, pulled the duvet tightly to her and flipped off the light. In the dark, he stumbled to the bathroom and pushed the door silently behind him. Locked it. Gazing into the mirror, he brushed his teeth slowly – rhythmically, powerfully, till his wrist grew tired. From the other room, he heard her coughing in her sleep. He spat into the sink, opened the tap, and let the water run. He watched it swirl through the drain. He knew why water ran clockwise in the north. In Australia it ran in the opposite direction. He thought of people on the other side of the world – people like him, gazing into mirrors in motel rooms on the other side of the world. He spat again and tossed the toothbrush in the bin.

*   *   *

She woke at eight and was out of bed in a second. She pulled at her clothes, packed her make-up. She reached for her cigarettes, lit one and inhaled deeply. Then she pulled on her cord jacket, slung her bag over her shoulder and marched from the room.

The car park was empty. Completely. She ran back to the room, flung open the door. "Sonny?"

She stood alone in the little room, shoved her fists deep into the pockets of her cord jacket, balled them into tight fists and straight away wished she'd worn her good coat.

Waiting for Alf

Judith Barrow

I ask her,
"What time is Alf coming?"
She answers,
"Soon, Ida, soon."

I try to stand, to check my hair in the mirror,
But fail.
My frailness surprises me –
But holds no terror.
Across the table Lily's still picking her nose.
"Your face'll cave in," I tell her.
Then see that the new feller has pissed himself.
Again!
I shout for the woman,

"When are you going to see to this one,
And what time will Alf get here?"

She ignores me.

Olga's crying.
Not really a cry – a drone;
A painful keening under her breath;
Mourning death: her own.

Gets on my nerves!

She's serving tea.
I grab her arm.

"What time is Alf coming?"
"Soon, Ida, soon."
I snort.
She's lying, you know,
She thinks I'm daft,
But if I say his name, he's still here
And the pain is easier to bear –
Just.

I must stand up!

Ivy's muttering,
Sylvia sings; brings memories to life.
The new chap, now dry,
Nods and snores.

The noise!

"Time to move."

I shove back the chair –
Push on the table,
Wait 'til I'm stable
Then, poised, look down.
My slippers are tight –
Are they on the wrong feet?
I screech for the woman.
She says no, they're right,
I ask, "When will Alf arrive?"

She doesn't answer,
So I pinch her.
"When will he arrive?"
And she replies,
"Soon, Ida, soon."

Silly cow!

Love in the Fast Lane

Jacqui Burns

"I don't know why I let you convince me to come here, Kim," I complained for the umpteenth time.

"Because if you didn't you'd be watching 'Midsomer Murders' in your jim-jams like you do every weekend."

"Okay," I conceded, "you have a point. But speed dating, I mean, it's just so not me!"

"How do you know if you haven't tried? Now cheer up. What do you want to drink?"

Picking up the drinks menu, I glanced down at the cocktails on offer. Each one included sex in the title and was a lethal concoction of at least three alcoholic drinks. I chose the Mind-blowing Orgasm on the Beach. I was filled with a sick feeling of dread for the evening ahead.

Since Martin and I had split up two years ago, I could count on one hand the number of times I'd been out. Taking Emily and Sarah to Brownies was the highlight of my social calendar. It felt safer indoors, indulging in my passion for Wagon Wheels, than launching myself on the dating scene.

I had to admit I'd let myself go. I was never going to be a tall, willowy blonde like Kim, but I'd given up making myself attractive. My legs were hairier than the Amazonian rainforest and the only thongs I owned were the sandals I wore in the summer.

Kim had gone to the toilet to touch up her lip-gloss and, perched inelegantly on the bar stool, I was conscious of my flabby stomach tucked into my Bridget Jones-style knickers.

"Penny for them." I looked up into the twinkling eyes of the barman as he handed over a luminous green cocktail.

"I was just wondering why I put myself through this." I grimaced as the tiny umbrella poked itself up one of my nostrils. "God, I've seen vomit a more attractive colour than this."

"We're a happy bunny tonight, aren't we?" he teased. "Look, it's only a bit of fun. You might actually enjoy it."

Kim returned and tugged on my arm, "Come on, it's about to start."

I flopped down at a small table, illuminated by a single candle. I braced myself for my first three-minute date. The card in front of me had two boxes. I had to place a tick for 'Would like to date' and a cross for 'Would not like to see again.' Nothing could be simpler.

My first date lowered himself nervously into the chair in front of me.

"I'm Colin and I work in a funeral parlour."

Colin had thin, sandy hair and large, unblinking eyes. He reminded me of those photo-fit pictures you see on "Crime Watch." I wondered why there wasn't a third box screaming, 'Never want to see again in a million years.'

Mark, thirty-four, seemed a better prospect. He was quite fanciable, for a start, and had curly black hair, which was greying sexily at the sides. When he told me he was an IT Consultant I made the fatal mistake of asking what it involved. I was treated to a detailed explanation for the rest of the three minutes.

Jerome, twenty-five, had blond highlights and skin the colour of a sun-dried tomato. His black shirt was unbuttoned to the navel to reveal a smooth, hairless chest. Within the first minute he asked if I liked threesomes. It was all I could do to stop myself from shouting 'Next!' in his face.

By the tenth date my head was spinning. All of the men had blended into one. The one thing they had in common was verbal incontinence. Each seized the opportunity to speak for the entire three minutes about themselves. Only Dominic (was he my fifth or sixth date?) asked me what I did. When I went on to tell him that I had two daughters, he began to fidget and spent the rest of our time looking over my shoulder at his next date.

Looking at my watch, I wondered if John Nettles had solved this week's murder. I felt like a schoolgirl waiting for the bell. Clearly, I wasn't ready for love in the fast lane. What was so wrong with limping along on the hard shoulder, anyway?

I raced for the bar during break. Tim, the barman, greeted me with another glass of luminous vomit.

"It can't have been that bad," he smiled.

"Wanna bet?" I insisted. He laughed when I went on to describe my dates from hell.

"Ohmigod!" Kim joined me at the bar. "What did you think of Jerome? Wasn't he gorgeous? He asked me to join him at his parents' villa in Ibiza this summer."

"In three minutes?" I raised my eyebrows.

"Yeah, well, the chemistry was right. What about you? Anyone you fancied?"

Tim leaned over, handing Kim her drink.

"I never was any good at chemistry," I said.

"You're too fussy," Kim argued.

The bell rang. With a sinking heart I realised it was time to meet my next dates.

"Only ten more to go," Tim grinned.

Needless to say, the next ten were no better than the first. The only light in the evening was watching Tim's broad shoulders behind the bar and drooling over his tight buttocks when he cleaned some tables nearby. Why had it taken me so long to realise that he was the only guy in the whole place worth flirting with?

When my ordeal was eventually over, I returned to the bar and gently eased off one of my shoes. "God, it's been a long night," I moaned.

"No one took your fancy, then?" Tim asked.

"Let's just say I won't even bother looking up the website to see if I have any matches."

Tim smiled and I noticed how his eyes crinkled in the corners.

"What about you? Ever endured a night like this?"

"Not really my style," he said. He glanced down at the colourful flyer propped up against the bar. "Anyway, Wednesday would be my night."

Intrigued, I let my eyes fall to the flyer. Alongside Wednesday night it read, 'Guys Meet Guys.' I smiled ruefully. All the evidence was there: he was good-looking, funny, not totally self-absorbed. Had to be gay.

"Want another drink?" Tim offered.

"Nah, there's a mug of Horlicks with my name on it at home." I looked over to Kim, who had her arms wrapped around Jerome. "Tell her I've gone, will you?"

Her Son

Kelly Fitzgerald

I killed my mom today. I didn't plan on doing it, but a couple of weeks ago she said she wanted me to go to college, find a good woman and be happy. I said I already was happy. Well, mostly. And I wasn't sure I wanted to go to college. So last week she didn't talk to me at all. She only howled and made everyone squirmy. Then this week she didn't say a word. I decided to do something about it. No one else was going to after all, because it was my choice to make, the doctors said.

The Photograph

Caroline Hawkes

It would take an hour for the photos to develop. Gardner didn't often come into town and he wasn't sure how to pass the time, but he'd parked the car in the cattle mart, on the outskirts, and didn't fancy doing the walk again. It was unfamiliar terrain. The concrete jarred his knees and the garish window dressings offended his eyes. He felt uncomfortable amongst the suited business people and the weekday shoppers.

For several minutes he looked at the window display in an outdoor pursuit shop. Rugged walking boots, with thick woolen socks wrinkled around their tops, had been placed underneath Teflon-coated jackets. There was a pile of twigs that Gardner supposed was a campfire, and placed next to it, a set of billy cans.

Across the street, a gentleman's outfitter caught his attention. He peered through yellow plastic sheeting at pinstripe suits, gaudy-looking ties and tight-fitting briefs. Gardner's clothes were all the same, or variations on a theme: thick or quilted chequered shirts, plain fleece jackets and jeans. For special occasions, he had a pair of dark brown cords. This was the clothing that he received for birthdays and Christmases, or things that his wife bought him. He was a practical person and he liked his clothes to be functional. Besides, if it was all the same, he didn't have to waste any time at the crack of dawn choosing something to wear. He never bought clothing for himself and wouldn't know where to start.

Gardner smiled at the thought of wearing one of the pinstripe suits, at the notion of unbuttoning the jacket and draping it over a gate, before rolling up the sleeves of an expensive white shirt and plunging his hand into the backside of a cow to grapple with a breech birth. He wondered what his wife might say, what the look on her face might be, if he took down his trousers to reveal a pair of tight-fitting briefs instead of his usual underwear.

A few weeks ago Gardner had picked up a hitchhiker at a motorway service station. It was a young man with a rucksack, who said that he was going to visit friends and that he was halfway through his journey. He seemed pleasant enough and they chatted at intervals for the thirty or so miles they travelled together – mostly small talk, niceties, a little about the weather and a little more about hitchhiking. Gardner dropped him off at a junction when their paths forked.

The following day, when Gardner was rummaging around in the passenger side of the car, he found a camera. It was just a snapper, an inexpensive point and shoot. For a moment he was confused as to where it had come from. When he realised that it must have belonged to the hitchhiker, Gardner did a strange thing. He became secretive, and instead of telling the story to his wife and showing her his find, he put the camera upstairs, in the back of his bedside drawer. It stayed there for weeks and every day Gardner had to look at it. The dial on the top indicated that twenty pictures had been taken and he was curious to see them. But being naturally cautious, he was reluctant to have the film developed in case it had some kind of criminal content and he was blamed. He could picture the headlines.

Last night, as he lay awake in the dark, he made up his mind. He would take it to the chemist on the high street, where his wife took her films to be processed. He would tell the assistant that he had found the film and would explain that he was developing it in an attempt to identify the owner. His innocence would be established from the start. He would make a bit of a joke of it, so the assistant would remember him, and would vouch for him, if the worst should happen. Gardner couldn't quite shift the uneasy feeling that he was stealing – an inherent wrong that had been instilled in him as a child. The fear of being caught, and the consequences that followed, had always dogged him.

In the morning, Gardner told his wife that he had a meeting. He put on his brown cords and a plain blue shirt, before shaving off a few days' worth of stubble. He held a comb under the hot tap before running it through his hair, sweeping it into a side parting. Finally, he directed a squirt of cologne toward the open neck of his shirt and brushed his teeth. He took the film out of the camera and put it in his jacket pocket.

*   *   *

Gardner moved away from the gentleman's outfitter because he started to feel a little conspicuous staring into the window. He imagined that he must stick out a mile and thought that everyone would be able to tell that he was a country boy. He wandered through the town, following the one-way system, until he came back to the chemist. There was still twenty minutes left, so he bought himself a takeaway coffee from a nearby café and sat down on the bench outside.

The young woman next to him was struggling to control a toddler. Every time she attempted to get the child into its pushchair the little boy made his body rigid so that he slipped out of it again. The child's face was contorted with rage and the woman was becoming more and more exasperated. Gardner didn't know why she didn't just leave him be and let him walk if that was what he wanted so badly, but then he didn't have children himself so didn't really feel qualified to comment.

His wife didn't want any children. She had told him that from the beginning and in fifteen years of marriage had yet to change her opinion. He had found her strength of mind attractive when they had first met. Gardner didn't have much experience with women and always had felt awkward in their company. When he was introduced to his wife and she asked to see him again, he was grateful that someone had chosen him, content to be able to stop looking and glad to settle down. It was never an all-consuming passion, but they shared a similar practical nature and a similar sense of humour. What Gardner had never known, he could never miss. Their relationship was comfortable. Like a pair of well-worn slippers, he often thought – nothing fancy, but easy to slip into at the end of a long day and easier still to live with.

As the time approached, Gardner could hardly believe how nervous he felt. His palms were sweating and despite the coffee, his mouth was still dry. He knew that he was behaving irrationally, but couldn't help it. He supposed that the main reason for his guilt was because he had kept something from his wife and he'd lied to her about where he was going. The ridiculousness of the situation wasn't lost on him. How many times had she asked him to pop into town for her? How many times had he refused, telling her, in all honesty, that he couldn't be doing with the place?

Gardner pushed open the door into the chemist. As it swung shut behind him, two damp handprints could be seen on the glass. He was aware of the security camera recording him as he crossed the shop floor. When he reached the counter, he handed his slip to the cashier with a slightly shaky hand. The woman appeared nonplussed as she set about retrieving his photographs from a bundle that had just been sent down from the lab. She frowned, hearing the man drumming his fingers on the counter behind her. She couldn't abide impatience and turned to look at him.

"Oh yeah, I remember now," she said. "You're the one that brought in that film you found."

"Er, yeah, that's right. I wanted to see if I could identify the owner so that I could return the camera." Gardner shifted from foot to foot. He felt that he'd been far too quick to reply and offered too much information.

She opened a larger packet, taking out the envelope of photographs. As she did this, a small piece of paper slipped out. Gardner gritted his teeth. The woman picked up the slip and Gardner watched her eyes scan the words.

"Looks like you're out of luck, love."

"What?"

"Note from the lab. Says that most of the photos have been overexposed."

"What does that mean?"

"It means, love, that they only managed to develop one of the

31

pictures. And I'm sorry, but I still have to charge you the full price."

Gardner exchanged his money for the slim envelope and left the shop. Just one photo. He was desperate to have a look at it, but deciding to get back to the car first, he put it in his inside pocket. He almost broke into a run, but managed to keep himself in check by reminding himself how foolish he must look. When he was back in the security of the car, with the noise and bustle of the town shut outside, he drew the envelope out of his pocket. He held his breath.

The photograph was a close-up shot of a woman's head and shoulders. The camera flash reflected off the straps of her silk dress. She had dark hair and a pearl choker around her throat. A slim and elegant arm, delicately kinked at the wrist, was holding an ornately decorated mask across the top half of her face. She was smiling, her lips stained red and slightly parted. The photograph stirred feelings in Gardner that he never knew existed. His skin prickled as the blood rushed through his veins in a way that he'd never been conscious of before. He almost felt his pupils dilate.

*   *   *

Catherine, Greta, Vivian. Gardner went through a list of classical Hollywood beauties of yesteryear. He felt compelled to name the woman in the photograph and wanted one that was fitting of her allure. He decided on Sophia. It sounded glamorous and he liked the way it felt in his mouth. It had a soft beginning that made you pout and the rest of the word popped out after it like a deep crimson plum. Sophia.

He kept the photograph in the inside pocket of his jacket. Every time he was alone he took it out and contemplated the face, the woman. Often, when he wasn't alone, he slipped his hand into his pocket and pressed his palm against the back of the picture. He was careful not to leave dirty smudges on the print. He didn't want her face to be more obscured than it already was. There were two almond-shaped holes in the mask, where the eyes should be. They were circled with small glittering gemstones. But beyond the holes lay an impenetrable darkness. It didn't matter how often Gardner strained to make out the possible colour of her irises; nothing could be discerned. But that was just another thrill, all part of the mystery.

The photograph, and the woman in it, touched the very essence of Gardner's soul. It spoke of another life, another world, where people didn't get up in the dark to milk cows and spent more than a fraction of a second deciding what to wear. This was the kind of woman that wouldn't look twice at Gardner, and now she belonged to him. He had her in his pocket and could gaze at her, without feeling self-conscious, whenever he wished.

He didn't see that he was doing anything wrong. It wasn't as though he was having an affair. He still behaved in exactly the same way toward his wife. Only now, when they hugged each other before going to bed at night, he smelled the nape of her neck and imagined that it was Sophia he was holding. But she wouldn't smell of Pears soap, like his wife did; Sophia would smell of an exotic and musky scent that she'd bought from a small perfumery in the back streets of Paris.

Nearly a month after Gardner had found and developed the photograph of Sophia, she disappeared. He was sure that he had left her in his coat pocket. He searched frantically, going through the car, his drawers and wardrobe, before turning out the pockets of every item of clothing that he owned – even the things that he hadn't worn for years. He looked in places where it was impossible for the photograph to be. He even lifted up the flap of loose carpet by the bedroom door. But it was no good. The panic burned in the centre of his chest, in the heart of his solar plexus. It took almost all of his energy to contain it, to prevent it from ripping through his ribcage and becoming something tangible. At one point his wife came into the bedroom and asked what he was looking for. He mumbled something about his wallet, without stopping to look at her face. He felt her presence in the doorway for several more minutes before she turned around and went back down the stairs. Gardner continued to search for another thirty-five minutes before admitting defeat. He had to stop himself from screaming and shouting, from kicking the doors and walls in frustration. Eventually he rubbed his hands over his face and went downstairs.

His wife was sitting at the kitchen table looking at the photograph. She wasn't crying and her face wasn't angry. She picked it up with her fingertips as if she could hardly bear to have it touch her skin. She tore it into eight pieces. The final tear was a struggle and the paper became mangled in the process. Without saying a word, she dropped the pieces onto the floor and left the room.

As soon as she disappeared from view, Gardner fell to his knees and began to gather the pieces. He scooped them up and slid them in between the pages of a newspaper. Later that evening, when his wife was in the bath, he crept into the bedroom and tucked the newspaper at the back of his bedside drawer. What he hadn't realised was that a scrap of the photograph had skittered across the lino and slipped underneath one of the worktops. In the darkness, the jewels that circled Sophia's eyes failed to gleam.

Lunch Breaks

Sandra Mackness

"Don't tell me you're off to watch the sea again, Lesley? It won't look any different from yesterday." Eric Johnson, chief accounts clerk, loomed over Lesley as she reached into her desk drawer for her lunchbox.

Lesley's smile slotted into place. Practised at batting off Eric's snide remarks, she said, "That's just where you're wrong, Eric. It's ever changing. That's the beauty of it."

Lesley was gone before Eric could wipe the grin from his fleshy features. A bit of company whilst he ate his packed lunch would have been good. One day, shortly after Lesley had joined the firm, he'd discovered her having her mid-day snack beside the photocopier as she watched press releases lumbering through. To his delight, on that occasion she'd exchanged one of her smoked ham and mozzarella sandwiches for one of his pressed pork.

"Are you interested in model railways by any chance?" he'd

asked her. But ever since then, for some strange reason, she'd chosen to keep to herself at lunchtime.

He retreated into his rabbit hutch of an office and unpacked his sandwiches: unappetizing rounds of two-day-old white bread. He sighed as he opened his newspaper. It was a pity Lesley wasn't friendlier, especially as he'd soon be moving from his bed-sit to a tastefully decorated terraced house just off the sea front. He considered asking her over for a bit of supper one evening after the move – might pull out the stops and get a tin of salmon and one of those mixed salad bags from Tesco's. After all, she must be missing male company, since her divorce.

His sausage-like fingers probed under the crusts to see if there was any cucumber or lettuce lurking, but no such luck. Dot Mackenzie, his landlady, had made the sandwiches for him and left them, mummified in greaseproof paper, outside his bedroom door. He hadn't wanted to offend her by refusing her offer of packed lunches, but now Dot was regularly waylaying him on his return from work in the evening.

"Have a good day then, Eric?" she'd say, cleavage heaving. "Want a cup of tea while I'm finishing your supper? The late Mr Mac always liked a nice cup of tea when he came in from work." And Eric couldn't help noticing that, since his arrival, Dot had changed her hair colour from a faded blonde to an unlikely shade of apricot.

Eric and his former wife Pauline had sold their marital home. He had been amazed when the woman he thought he knew well informed him she wanted a divorce.

"You can have custody of the train sets, Eric," she'd said icily. "It will be a relief not to hear those engines rumbling."

Stung, Eric had just stared at her.

"I'm moving in with someone else," she'd told him. Then she hauled two packed suitcases from under the stairs and let herself out through the front door. Eric watched her get into a flashy car. At the wheel was a man Eric recognised as the Entertainments Manager from the leisure breaks complex just up the coast. And to think he'd paid for Pauline to accompany him on a long weekend's model railway convention several months before. Eric watched as the man planted a smacker on Pauline's lips. They drove off into the sunset, leaving Eric alone with his model railway.

Pauline moved into the Entertainments Manager's luxury en-suite double chalet and was no doubt enjoying full house every night.

Now Eric was about to move into a new place in Peel Bay. Alone in his office, he reran his favourite fantasy of a rosy future where Lesley did meaningful things in his kitchen. He would, of course, be playing with his piston engine in the front room.

"Casserole's simmering nicely, darling. It's beef in stout," Lesley trilled from within Eric's subconscious. "Mashed potato or rice, darling?"

A large dollop of mashed potato, Eric mouthed. He ran his tongue over his lips. His gold-rimmed spectacles steamed up as he chomped his way through the white bread and rubbery liver sausage.

*   *   *

Spray slapped viciously against the pier struts. The receding tide left a strip of clattering damp shingle. Sludgy-green bladders of seaweed clung to wet rocks. As Lesley unwrapped her sandwiches, a beady-eyed seagull watched. It was a blustery day and she was glad of the sturdy Perspex windbreak that shielded the municipal bench.

She glanced to her left. He was there again, the fair-haired man who'd been eating his lunch at the adjoining bench every day for the last three weeks. Maybe he was a fresh air fiend. Certainly there was never anyone else around, except the dog walkers, hurrying or strolling along, depending on the weather and the size of their dog. Lesley and the man sometimes exchanged nods and smiles when she passed his bench on her way back to the office.

Once they almost fell into step when they'd risen simultaneously from their benches, but after self-conscious smiles, they both went their respective ways. Lesley liked the look of his shy grin and would have liked to chat with him, but it seemed the opportunity was lost.

Peel Harbour in early December: the rock and candyfloss stalls were long gone, the deckchairs stored away till Easter. At this time of year it was possible to enjoy the sight and sound of the choppy sea and to have an uninterrupted view of the little ferry that appeared daily at half-past one, shouldering its way across the bay.

Today, Lesley munched her BLT on multi-grain bread. She wondered what the man on the next bench was eating for his lunch. There was probably a Mrs Man to prepare his sandwiches. Somehow he had that married look.

I'd better go back, she sighed to herself, brushing crumbs from her lap on to the promenade. A large seagull glared at the pittance she left behind but Lesley was already walking away, her shiny dark hair lifted from her face by the breeze.

Lesley's departure reminded the man on the next bench that he too must go. He watched her red jacket's progress up the steps to the pavement and toward the big office block just off the sea front.

The man had seen her go in on several occasions. He thought she looked friendly. It would be so good to talk to someone friendly, he mused. His job in the Benefits Office was sometimes quite stressful, when clients challenged his calculations.

It was odd, but he didn't miss Jenny.

"I don't think we've got a future together, Rob. Not any more. I think we both know that really." They had never got around to marriage and as soon as she'd spoken, Rob knew she was only voicing his own fears about their relationship. Jenny's relief when he agreed it was time to move on had confirmed his suspicions that she had already found a replacement for him.

Now he longed to find someone he could feel at ease with and have fun with. It was so difficult to meet new people. The woman who ate her lunch on the next bench looked about his age. A sinking feeling struck him as he considered the probability that she was already in a relationship.

The following week, Lesley and Rob were both absent from their benches as rain drowned Peel Bay. It drummed on the promenade and drenched the Christmas trees erected by the Council. Streetlights, crowned with festive set pieces, poured fruit-gum colours on to the dank pavements and a six-foot Santa complete with sledge and team of prancing reindeer lit up the sea front. Luckily for Lesley, Eric Johnson had the week off to move into his new house.

"Would you believe I needed thirty-nine boxes to pack all my train sets when my stuff went into storage?" he'd informed Lesley.

But the next week dawned mild and clear, with a gentle breeze teasing the striped pennant on top of the bandstand. Senior citizens, coats buttoned up under their chins, sauntered along the prom or sat over skinny lattés and chocolate muffins in Starbucks.

"This is more like it," they agreed.

Lesley left the office at top speed on Monday at one o'clock. To her dismay, Eric Johnson, testosterone-fuelled and fanciful, had honed in on her, his aftershave preceding him.

"How about a cup of coffee at lunchtime, Les?"

Lesley, tapping out a memo, had suddenly started typing gibberish. Panicking, her excuse for refusing his tempting offer was that she was meeting a friend for lunch.

All she could think of as she left the building was to head straight for the fair-haired guy's bench instead of her own. When he arrived, she would apologise for intruding on his privacy and ask if he would pretend to be her friend for half an hour. Eric the Eager would soon slope off if he'd been following her. It was bad enough to be newly divorced and with your self-esteem in shreds, without having a stalker.

But today of course, the man didn't arrive. Wouldn't you just know it? Lesley opened her lunchbox with trembling fingers, keeping her head down as she took out an egg and cress sandwich. She waited on the unfamiliar bench, dreading seeing a triumphant Eric Johnson materialise beside her to ask if she'd been stood up.

The fair-haired man arrived at Lesley's usual bench a few yards away and sat down. He stared out to sea, dejected by the woman's non-appearance. And, in his determination to see her, he'd left his lunch on his desk.

Just my luck. Rob had been psyching himself up for this all morning, having figured he had nothing to lose. Soon they would both be forced to find another lunchtime spot anyway. After Christmas, gales and chilly dank fogs would swirl around the bay.

But Lesley shifted her position, jolting Rob out of his reverie. His sideways glance showed her sitting on his usual bench, snuggled into her red fleecy jacket. He stood up and in a few strides of his long legs, was standing in front of her.

"Who's been sitting on my bench?" he asked. "Oh God, that's a terrible chat-up line," he apologised.

Their relieved laughter was snatched away by the salty breeze. A waiting gull hovered near the sea wall, flaps down and ready to swoop. As Lesley and Rob began walking to the nearby Starbucks, a man in a khaki anorak appeared from behind the bandstand. Unfortunately for the seagull, Eric Johnson homed in on Lesley's leftover sandwiches and began to munch. Then he took out his model railway collectors' magazine from his pocket and opened it at the readers' letters page.

The Vixen

David Jones

The winding walkway parted 'neath the shade
Of boulder rock on bluebell eiderdown.
She stood in frozen silence in the glade,
An effigy of beauty unbeknown.
Her terracotta brush concealed a trace
Of battle wounds and scars from hidden snare.
Her glinting glance transfixed upon my face
Behind her demure stance and solemn stare.
A lonely ray of sunshine then appeared,
A spotlight on the leading lady fair.
And then arose the melody she feared,
A voluntary trumpet in the air.
A final look and ultimate goodbye,
She vanished through the shadow of my eye.

Summer's Love

Nadine Fry

Somewhere in the distance a siren sounded. The noise sent a chill down my spine. After all this time, the sound still disturbed me. Whether from police or ambulance, it had the haunting wail of pain and suffering.

A graceful white butterfly fluttered past the open window where I sat gazing out at our garden. A warm breeze blew in and the light, airy curtains billowed like sails into the cool room behind me, almost blocking me from view, should anyone have been there.

I sat on my window seat, legs stretched out before me, tanned and golden. Then I shifted slightly to a more comfortable position. I smiled as my silver, glitter nail-polish twinkled in the sun; my daughters favourite – "fairy dust, Mummy," she'd say in her sweet voice, "this will help you fly."

I smiled once more at the memory, and glanced out of the open side window into the garden, just in time to see my daughter give

43

one final spin, before falling to the floor in a heap. I could hear her infectious, throaty laughter as she lay on the grass, dizzily staring up at the endless, blue sky.

The flowers in the garden were in full bloom; a rainbow of colours nodded their delicate heads in the breeze. The trees were green and lush and their branches spread over the lawn, casting sun-speckled shadows invitingly, as if calling out for someone to come and sit under them. It was July and the middle of summer, my favourite time of year. Also, the season my daughter was born; my Summer, named when she entered this world scarlet and screaming one beautiful August afternoon.

And there she was, six years later, one whole year after the accident, spinning and skipping, as her dress spun and danced with her, racing around our huge cherry-blossom tree. As she ran, I could see the soles of her feet, stained a deep green from her prancing and dancing on the freshly mown lawn. In a flash of long, blonde curls she appeared from around the tree and looked toward me. She put her small hand to her lips and blew me a kiss. I put up my hand, as if to catch it – something we always did if we weren't close enough to touch.

The accident seemed so close, it could have happened yesterday. It was all over so quickly; at the time it seemed a blur. But not now, now I could remember every detail: every second, every smell, every colour, everything. Like a video tape being played over and over in my mind, making me go through it over and over again in slow-motion, trying to make me remember something, something I may have been able to change.

It had been so warm that day, the last day of the school term. Summer and I were walking along the narrow pavement, laughing and chatting about the school fete we had just been to, tickling and

44

teasing each other. I had been holding her hand so tight; she was making faces because our held hands were sweating from the heat. I swear, I'd just let her go for a second, so I could wipe my sticky hands on the seat of my shorts. She was in the middle of the road before I could take a breath, both hands outstretched as her silver helium balloon drifted even further from reach.

It had been her prize at the 'hook a rubber duck' stall. She'd been laughing uncontrollably as the plastic ducks had wobbled this way and that. She'd finally hooked one on her stick – her prize a chocolate frog or a balloon. She'd chosen the pretty silver balloon, as the frog would melt on the way home and she couldn't eat it yet as she'd just eaten a giant hot dog with "loads of burnt onions, please!"

Summer stood there as the car came around the corner. She looked at the car and then at me as I dashed to the edge of the road, my hands clamped over my mouth. That moment is frozen in time, embedded in my memory forever: Summer standing there in a yellow vest-top and denim pedal-pushers, her silky blonde hair in two French plaits, blue bows dangling on the ends. Standing there like a frightened fawn, her enormous, blue eyes wide, not knowing whether to go forward or back.

I screamed a gut-wrenching scream, a scream that woke me from nightmares for many months later. But it was too late. The car hit and my tiny baby doll lay broken on the road, just yards from the car that had tried to scream to a halt, but failed.

The paramedics had worked on my little girl, as I stood numb while the lady driver sobbed hysterically. How I wish we'd picked a chocolate frog that day instead of a silver balloon.

The sound of our tall, iron gates gently whining open brought me to the present, and as the nose of my husband's car purred into

45

the driveway I saw him look over to the cherry-blossom tree where our daughter always played, as she jumped up and down waving frantically at her father.

Maybe this time he would see her, but he looked away and drove on. As he came closer I could see the tears running down his face, as they did every day when he looked to the tree and saw his little girl was no longer there.

Summer looked at me, a sad smile on her rosebud lips. I smiled back to reassure her, one day he would see her, just like I do now, when the time is right. The guilt and the nightmares would stop and he would see our precious angel once again, and this time nothing would take her away – not even death.

I looked over to my daughter as she stood under the tree, her hair and dress blowing gently in the breeze, and put my hand to my lips and blew her a kiss. She smiled as she reached into the air and caught it.

Slow Suicide

Ansley Moon

Alcohol was his poison.
Fatal for him. He'd purse
his lips against
a bottle and feel the
strong liquid blaze
his throat. Over
the years it coursed
through his body.
Each birthday
flooding another organ:
his liver, his brain, but
most notably
his heart.

What Not To Get Your Girlfriend

Nicky Herriot

It started with a phone call – but then, doesn't it always?

"Hey I've got it, got the Sims computer game and one of the add-ons, and it's great, I've already installed it, and guess what, the best bit is you can have two women living together in the same house, I've got lesbians living in the same house, it's great...are you still there?"

"Yes," I replied, with a smile in my voice. I'd been a little distracted, trying to see if there had been any full stops in her sentence. "So, you are having fun with it?" I like computers; I use them for work, love all the anti-virus and anti-hacking stuff, love fixing them, but I can't get the games addiction like some women I know.

"Yes," she said, but I could already hear that she was drifting off, wanting to get back to her new people.

*   *   *

I got another phone call the next night.

"It's all falling apart," she said. "They won't sleep together. I can't get them both into bed, and since there's only one bed, the other one has to sleep on the couch. One of them is always late for work because I just can't get her up in time in the morning. And I'm trying to build up their relationship points, but the one sleeping in the bed is cross with the other one because she isn't doing any housework."

"Sounds like a proper relationship to me," I replied.

"And the one on the couch is depressed. I had to make her lose her job because..."

"Hang on," I interrupted, "you had to make her lose her job? Why? How?" Oh dear, was I getting hooked?

"When they were both at work there was no time to clean the house and they were unhappy all the time," she continued.

"So why did she lose her job and not the other one?"

"I can't have the police officer lose her job, she looks so cool in her uniform."

*   *   *

Then I got a phone call at one o'clock in the morning.

"There's been a fire in the kitchen!"

"WHAT?" I yelled, leaping out of my bed to rescue her.

"In my Sims house, there was a fire in the kitchen. The one who is unemployed can't cook. I'm trying to get her to learn to cook but she keeps saying she's too depressed. So, she set fire to the kitchen and the brigade had to come and put it out. And I still can't get

49

them into bed with each other. The working one is depressed, too, because she can't wash her dishes."

"Why not?" I asked, knowing I was going to regret the answer.

"The other woman fell asleep on the floor, in front of the sink, because I forgot to send her to bed. She started crying and then she wet herself because I didn't send her to the toilet in time," she replied. "I tried boosting their social points so I thought one of them could phone a friend for a chat. But I forgot to check the time and her friend slammed the phone down on her because it was 3 a.m. She lost lots of social points."

I could relate to that I thought, looking at the clock.

* * *

I phoned one of my friends, looking for support.

"Sims is great," Kim replied. "You can build cities, design houses, control people."

Never phone a Virgo for Sims support, I thought, as I hung up.

* * *

It was quiet until Saturday morning.

A very happy voice said, "Hey, I got them into bed. I've done it."

"How?" I replied, looking at the empty side of my bed and thinking I could get some tips… from a computer game?

"I moved the wardrobe. Apparently the wardrobe was in her way, so she couldn't physically get into the bed."

I looked around my bedroom, debating the worth of throwing my furniture out the window. I doubted it would work for me.

"Now they're very happy. They're going to try for a baby!"

*   *   *

The baby arrived the next day – adopting babies for a lesbian couple is apparently very easy in the computer world. I still got the phone calls though.

"I'm going to have to get the social services to take the baby away," she said. "They can't get any sleep, their relationship is suffering, the baby is always crying and the house is a mess."

Ah, the Sims world is like the real world.

"How's your real life getting on?" I asked. "Seen your girlfriend recently?" Oh God, do I sound sarcastic?

"Ah, yes," she replied, "do you fancy coming around for dinner tonight? I need you to look at the computer. It seems a bit slow."

"I'll be there," I promised, getting out of bed to find that disc with a computer virus on it.

* First published in *Diva*, 2003.

It's Friday – So It Must Be Fish

Judith Barrow

INTRO MUSIC: CLIFF RICHARD – WE DON'T TALK ANY MORE.

SETTING: STAGE DIVIDED INTO TWO HALVES.

HER – SITTING ROOM OF SMALL COUNCIL HOUSE, CROWDED WITH FURNITURE. SHE IS SITTING ON THE SETTEE, SMOKING AND DRINKING.

HIM – SPARSLEY FURNISHED KITCHEN. HE IS MOVING AROUND, EMPTYING SHOPPING BAGS, PREPARING A MEAL, FRYING FOOD ETC AND DRINKING TEA.

HER: Apparently it was the fish that did it.

HIM: That fish was the final straw.

HER: Personally, I can't stand fish, but he insisted that's what he wanted, fish, every Friday. And I always had to go into town for it, to the market. He said it was the only place to get decent fish. And it always had to be sea bass. Ugh, horrible; slimy. I wouldn't touch it.

HIM: It was the only thing I ever asked her for. Nothing else. I'd long since stopped expecting anything else. (PAUSE) She always made such a fuss about having to get the bus but it was the only time she did have to use public transport; she had the car every weekend. And the buses are every hour on the hour, so I could never see what the problem was … except it meant leaving the bloody dogs on their own for a while.

HER: Oh, he wouldn't let me have the car during the week, oh no. He said he needed it, just in case one of his old folks had to be taken somewhere. So I had to leave my dogs alone. Here they are, Georgie, Annabelle; (DOGS BARKING) beautiful Chihuahuas, (HIGH PITCH TONE) aren't you, sweeties? I show them – Georgie especially – I've been all over the country with him. (LOW) Not so much with Annabelle. She's a bit short in the leg, so I've only been to local shows with her, but still, (HIGH PITCH TONE) she usually comes best in her class, don't you darling? As I said, Friday mornings I always had to leave them for over two hours by themselves. They'd pine, you know, especially Georgie. And then when I came home, he'd sulk. Georgie, I mean, not him. Mind you, he can sulk, he could sulk for Wales!

HIM: She only ever talks about her dogs. She just goes on and on about them all the time; Georgie and Annabelle, silly bloody names for daft bloody dogs. They're like damned rugs, always underfoot. Even so, I've always tried to show an interest, always listened when she'd been to the competitions and such.

HER: And not a bit interested in anything I had to say.

HIM: She knows I need the car in the week. She's just ashamed of what I do – says it's a woman's job, home helping, but I can't see her doing it. My clients don't have four legs. (PAUSE) I like my work. It's mostly men I see to; they're glad when I call and we have a good chat about all sorts of things. Not just dogs. A long time ago… it was nineteen eighty, after it all happened, we talked… in those days we did talk, about getting a pet. I wanted a couple of cats. I love cats, they're quiet, independent and they let you know exactly what they want just by the way they look at you. I thought we could have two, so they could keep one another company while we were both out at work… but she decided to get a dog and that's what we've had for the last twenty-four years. Dogs. I hate them, yap, yap, yapping and no mind of their own.

MUSIC: CLIFF RICHARD – WE DON'T TALK ANYMORE

HER: It was after I lost the baby, all those years ago; that's when he changed, got more moody. I don't really know why, because at the time he said he'd never wanted a family anyway.

HIM: That wasn't a good time. She was in a bad way, blamed herself. I'd always wanted kids but I told her it didn't matter; we had each other … then. I never mentioned it again.

HER: He'd never sulked before … not that I can remember anyway.

(OFF STAGE) CLANG OF LETTER BOX. DOGS BARK.

HER: (STUBBING OUT CIGARETTE AND CALLING) Georgie … Annabelle. (STANDING UP) It was his idea to get a pet, so I surprised him and brought home a dog. She was a Chihuahua, too: Clarissa … He never really took to her either.

HIM: (STANDING STILL AND DRINKING TEA) So, last Friday I said, where's the fish? I always cooked it; it wasn't as if I ever asked her to do anything with it. It was the one decent meal in the week I had, if I say so myself. She charcoals everything. She says 'it's a little bit touched,' in that whiny voice of hers. (PAUSE) It's always bloody cinderised!

SHE LEAVES THE ROOM. RETURNS WITH AN ENVELOPE AND STANDS STILL.

HER: Anyway, last Friday, Georgie was ill; he's got a delicate stomach and I think he'd picked something up from next door. (PAUSE) That's the trouble with these kinds of estates; they're what they call 'open plan.' What it is, really, is the Council's just saving money, not bothering to put up proper fences. (SITTING DOWN) Georgie, don't do that to your sister, it's not nice. Anyway, next door they're always throwing stuff out for the birds, lumps of bacon and the like. The birds never touch it. I've told them, it just goes rancid; it'll bring rats. (PAUSE) They take no notice.

Ignorant! I don't talk to them now. (PATTING SETTEE) Come on, up, up. Good dogs! So, on Friday, I didn't get to the market. I nipped to the Spar round the corner; got him cod in batter – not just ordinary batter, mind. According to the packet it was a new recipe: 'beer batter – crisp and light' it said. I thought it would make a change. I told him, you can still cook it yourself. He always says I can't cook fish. I told him once; I'll cook anything but fish.

HIM: Always bloody cinderised!

HER: I'm a good cook, I said. Just tell me what you want … And, you know, I didn't just mean food. Tell me what you want, I said. (PAUSE) He never did.

HIM: She's like a damn record, going on and on. I shut off.

HER: Sometimes it's as though I'm talking to a brick wall. I say, we don't have dialogue, you
and me. I have monologues. He never answers.

HE SETS TABLE, PUTS FISH ON PLATE AND SITS DOWN, STARTS TO EAT.

HIM: She never went back to work.

HER:(LIGHTING ANOTHER CIGARETTE) We'd waited ten years before we decided to start a family; it never seemed to be the right time, what with him building up the business, finding just the right house… exotic holidays. We'd two cars in those days: sports models, of course. He'd show off about them to his mates. He had friends then. (PAUSE) There wasn't time to think about children … well, to be honest, it wasn't really something we'd discussed. It wasn't planned. Suddenly I was pregnant. (PAUSE) After the miscarriage, they said I wouldn't be able to have another baby; there were complications, so I had to have a hysterectomy. Settle down, you two. I felt bad – guilty for some reason. I couldn't face going back to work again. (PAUSE) He suggested getting a pet and that gave me the idea. (OPENS LETTER AND READS IT, THEN STUBS OUT CIGARETTE, SITS BACK) I'd always liked Chihuahuas and I saw this programme about dog shows so I thought, that's what I'll do, dog breeding, showing, I even built up a reputation for grooming – only for the right people, useful people, if you know what I mean. He encouraged me then. If he resented it, he should have said. (PAUSE, LIGHTING ANOTHER CIGARETTE) He poked that fish around as if I was trying to poison him.

HIM: (CHEWING) She should have got them by now.

HER: (FLAPPING PAPER) Divorce papers.

HIM: (PUTTING KNIFE AND FORK DOWN AND SITTING BACK IN CHAIR) Bloody packet fish in batter. It was sodding disgusting. (PAUSE) I gave it to the dog. He was sick all over her. I said it's your own fault, you shouldn't have picked him up. We had a row. She said she hated living in that house and she hated the neighbours. I told her, if she'd helped more with the business, spent less on the bloody dogs, it wouldn't have all gone down the pan and we wouldn't have lost the other place with its 'useful' neighbours. Or the cars. (PAUSE) I suppose you think me daft, getting so worked up about a piece of fish, but it was the principle of the thing, you understand. The only real decision I made for myself on the domestic front. She's always organised everything else in our lives. She even chose what friends we had. Well, it says it all. Where are they all now? (POURING AND DRINKING MORE TEA) She's never been bothered about doing this last house up.

HER: (STUBBING OUT CIGARETTE, CRYING) My life's revolved around him ever since we were first married. I've done everything for him but it's never been enough. I tried to help him with the business from Day One, you know, paperwork and so on, but he didn't want me to be involved, said he had a secretary for all that and, anyway, I'd make a mess of it. He said just because I'd worked in an office, it didn't mean I knew everything about getting a car franchise and running a showroom. (BLOWING NOSE) I told him, I never said I did. But I could have learned! (STANDING UP, WALKING ABOUT, TAKING BOTTLE FROM SIDEBOARD AND WALKING BACK TO SETTEE) He's never been the same since he went bankrupt and we came to this god-forsaken place. I'd be ashamed for anyone to come here, so I made sure they didn't. It wasn't too difficult; people get offended over the slightest things. We didn't need them anyway; not any more. (SITTING DOWN, BLOWING NOSE) He's so involved in that stupid job, he works all hours, far more than he gets paid for. Still, (PATTING HER LAP) up, up … I've always got my dogs.

HIM: I might as well not have been there.
HER: He doesn't need me; he lost interest in me ages ago.

58

HIM: We've had nothing in common for years. At first I thought, even if I didn't like them, the dogs would be good for her. But she became obsessed, forever fussing over them. I got sick of finding dog hairs all over the furniture, in the shower, on the bed. Especially on the bed. (GRINNING) I'd kick the mutts off when she wasn't looking. (PAUSE) I can't remember the last weekend she was home – always traipsing round the country to meetings and dog shows. I've felt shut out from her life for a long time.

HER: (WIPING EYES) I've stood by him all these years.

HIM: I've felt lonely for years.

HER: I had no idea things were so bad. He never said anything, only the usual moaning about the money spent on the dogs and I always ignored that. (POURING DRINK) I'll never forget the day he came home and told me the business was going bankrupt, that we'd lost the house and everything. He looked dreadful. I wanted to put my arms around him and hold him but before I could, he went off to the study and shut himself in. (DRINKS) He stayed there nearly two days. Drinking! The telephone kept ringing but he wouldn't talk to anyone. I kept knocking on the door; I was so scared he'd do something stupid. In the end I just stopped answering the phone.

HIM: (STANDING UP) The business had been struggling for a while; the punters weren't buying. Then the accountant told me we were too exclusive, we should diversify, expand to include secondhand, but it was too late. I lost heart. (PICKS UP PLATE,

PUSHES CHAIR BACK) I tried talking to her, told her to keep a rein on the spending, but she took no notice. You should have seen her face when I told her what we were going through. Like... like... I disgusted her... she couldn't wait for me to get out of her sight. I don't remember much about those first few days; I think I drank quite a bit... worst time of my life... well, second worst.

HER: He left me to deal with everything. In the early days he'd had me sign all sorts of papers, put me down as one of the directors of the firm. Because of that, our accountant insisted I got involved, said I had to move fast before the creditors got to know how bad things were. I went to the showrooms to tell his staff what had happened. I think they all knew anyway, which was more than I did. I helped the secretary sort through the records and such. She was a nice girl – I was sorry I'd resented her all those years. (PAUSE) She cried a lot. When he did finally emerge from his bolthole I got no thanks.

HIM: (TAKES PLATE ETC. TO SINK) Sheer bloody panic set in when she realised it was the end of the good life. 'Course she had to start organising things before the dust had even settled. I might have been able to salvage something if she hadn't interfered, but it was too late by the time I realised what she was doing. She'd already started the process of registering the firm as insolvent; said the accountant had told her what to do. I said I bet he got his bloody fees sorted out first.

HER: I've been his whipping boy ever since.

HIM: (BEGINNING TO WASH UP) It's been downhill for us ever since.

HER: (LIGHTS CIGARETTE, BLOWS SMOKE OUT, DRINKS, SHRUGS) I can't eat, can't sleep. Know this isn't good for me, but so what. (PUTS GLASS DOWN, LEANS FORWARD) Anything goes wrong and it's my fault. This place doesn't help... it's claustrophobic. It was all the council could offer. They said when something else turned up we could apply for it. Now they say we don't have enough points or something to get a bigger place, so we've been stuck here five years, falling over one another. It's like a rabbit hutch. I'm just glad I get away weekends.

HIM: (CONTINUING TO WASH UP, CLEAR AWAY) I hated that place as much as she does, but she's never tried to adjust. I've moved on. You have to forget what was and live for now. This job's taught me that, at least. She's carried on doing exactly what she wants to, gallivanting around with the dogs, never mind where the money comes from. Well, she's going to have to learn.

HER: Out of the blue he says I'm leaving you.

HIM: I've been renting this flat for three months now.

HER: Left me without a penny to my name.

HIM: Been coming here in the evenings ... told her I'd extra hours to do.

HER: I've hardly seen him for months. I'd be in bed by the time he got home. All that overtime, and he gave me nothing.

HIM:Gave me a break from her infernal nagging. I'd stay as late as I could and then go home to sleep.

HER: I've no idea where he's gone.

HIM: I'll be ok here.

HER: I just don't know what I'm going to do.

HIM: I suppose you could say it was lack of communication – she's never learned how to listen.

HER: He just won't talk to me.

HIM: (OPENS A CUPBOARD, GETS OUT A BOTTLE OF WHISKY, SITS DOWN, POURS A DRINK) I suppose I could have carried on, but once I'd told her I was leaving, once I'd said it, I couldn't go back. Not really.

HER: He'll come back, tail between his legs…

HIM: (DRINKS, PAUSES) … could I?

HER: (LIGHTS ANOTHER CIGARETTE, POURS A DRINK) … won't he?

LAST FEW BARS - MUSIC: CLIFF RICHARD – WE DON'T TALK ANYMORE

CURTAIN

Dial

Dian Jenkins

Nos Wener, ac roedd lolfa'r Bedol Arian yn orlawn yn ôl yr arfer. Roedd hi'n unarddeg o'r gloch a phawb bron yn gwegian wedi oriau o yfed.

Chwarddodd grwp o ddynion wrth y bar wrth glywed un o'u cwmni yn adrodd stori ddoniol arall. Doedd Llŷr byth yn brin o jôc neu ddwy, ac ar ôl yfed gormod, fe fyddai'r storiau'n mynd yn fwy diwardd ac yntau'n fwy digywilydd a llac ei dafod nes yn y diwedd i rai ddweud wrtho am gau ei geg. Ond i'r gweddill arwr oedd e a dyma nhw'n ei gocso 'mlaen.

"Ti'n gwybod beth Llŷr, ti'n gwastraffu dy amser yn gweithio gyda'r Gwerthwyr tai 'na. Galle ti wneud dy ffortiwn yn mynd o amgylch y clybiau a'chan," meddai un.

"Too bloody right," meddai un arall, gyda'r lleill yn brefu eu cytundeb fel praidd o ddefaid gwirion.

"Dwed nawr te," gofynnodd un arall, "ble wyt ti' n clywed y storiau 'ma neu a wyt ti'n adrodd o brofiad?"

"Ffycin hell," medd aelod arall o'r grwp. "Os wyt ti, s'dim un ferch yn saff yn y dre' 'ma, a ti'n blydi lwcus fyd 'na gyd sy 'da fi i'w ddweud, ti'n mynd drwyddyn nhw mewn chwinciad."

Chwarddodd y lleill yn afreolus cyn archebu rownd arall o gwrw. Roedd Llŷr, erbyn hyn, yn cael gwaith sefyll ar ei draed ond doedd dim eisiau llawer o berswâd arno i ddechrau ar ei ddegfed peint o lager. Roedd y cwmni a'r ganmoliaeth wedi ei ysbrydoli. Galwodd ei ffrindiau ato, cododd wynt yn uchel, sychodd yr ewyn o'i swch gyda'i lawes a dywedodd "un stori to cyn i fi gael pisad."

"A glywoch chi am y fenyw 'na yn y washeteria? Wedd hi wedi cael ei dal yn fyr, a we rhaid iddi rhoi ei nicers yn y mashin. Daeth y dyn 'ma mewn â Alsation mowr 'da fe…"

"Ca dy ben Llŷr," gorchmynnodd Guto. "Mae menywod yn 'iste draw fanna."

"O Gut a'chan. A we'n rhaid i ti sarnu'r stori? Gai ddweud honna rhywbryd to pan fydd y gwdi gwdi "ma adre" yn cael swc "da mami," dywedodd Llŷr yn chwerw gan gyfeirio at Guto, ei ffrind gorau ers oedden nhw'n blant bach yn ysgol y dref.

Bu tipyn o genfigen rhyngddyn nhw ers yr amser hynny, y ddau yn awyddus i fod yn geffyl blaen. Erbyn hyn, â'r ddau'n ugain a mwy, roedd y sefyllfa wedi gwaethygu gydag un yn ceisio maeddu'r llall ym mhob ffordd bron – pwy fyddai'n pasio'i brawf gyrru'n gyntaf; pa un fyddai'n siafio'n gyntaf; pa un fyddai'n cael wejen go iawn, a chysgu gyda hi ac erbyn hyn, pa un oedd wedi cysgu gyda'r mwyafrif o ferched.

Ni fyddai Llŷr, y mwyaf hyderus a golygus o'r ddau, byth yn brin o ferch ddeniadol. Byddai'n eu swyno gyda'i lygaid tywyll, ei amrannau melfed, ei wefusau llawn addewid ac yn aml ei dafod brwnt. Roedd Guto, ar y llaw arall, yn swil ac yn ddihyder ei ffordd. Bachgen diymhongar, caredig a feddyliai mwy am gymeriad a theimladau merch nac am ei pharodrwydd i gysgu gydag ef. Byddai'n casau gweld Llŷr yn trin a thrafod merched yn wael a byddai'n aml yn dweud wrtho am eu parchu'n fwy.

"Ffyc 'em and chuck 'em, a 'mlaen at yr un nesa' Gut, mae digon mas 'na all panting for it," byddai ei ymateb. "And we've got it," chwarddodd Llŷr wrth roi pwt i Guto rhwng ei goesau.

Roedd hynny'n wir i raddau, ond o'r holl ddewis oedd ar gael, fe ddaru'r ddau ffansio'r un ferch. Guto ai gwelodd yn gyntaf. Y diwrnod hwnnw, aeth Guto allan o weithdŷ'r garej lle roedd yn dysgu'i grefft, i brynu baget o bopty newydd ei hagor gerllaw. Y tu ôl i'r cownter roedd merch a ddaeth i fod yn gannwyll ei lygaid mewn rhai wythnosau. Doedd e erioed wedi bod yn hapusach, a hithau hefyd i'w gweld, yn ei addoli. Ond bu Guto mor ddwl â chyflwyno Angharad i Llŷr ryw noson yn y Bedol Arian. Gwelodd Guto ei ffrind yn ei llygadu a phan aeth Angharad i'r tŷ bach, dywedodd Llŷr 'neis iawn Gut, tipyn o bishyn wir. Ydy hi cystel â'i golwg, ah?"

"Paid â siarad mor frwnt ambwyti Angharad," dwrdiodd Guto. "Mae'n ferch deidi. Fyddai dim gwahaniaeth 'da fi i setlo lawr 'da Angharad," ychwanegodd Guto.

Edrychodd Llŷr arno fel petai wedi tyfu cyrn.

"Ffycin hell Gut, byddi di'n mynd i Mothercare i brynu bwtis a bibs cyn bo' hir os na fyddi di'n ofalus," chwarthodd Llŷr gan roi hwp i ysgwydd ei ffrind nes ei fod yn sarnu ei lager dros y ford.

Ond roedd Llŷr wedi ffansio Angharad a hithau'n gwrido o dan ei edrychiad gwerthfawrogol. Ymhen ychydig wythnosau, roedd cannwyll llygad Guto wedi ei diffodd a'i wejen fach neis wedi troi ei chefn arno a sylweddolodd ei bod hi a Llyr erbyn hyn, yn eitem go iawn. O'r eiliad honno, trodd y genfigen rhyngddynt yn gasineb pur. Byddai'r ddau yn pryfocio ei gilydd am y peth lleiaf, a Guto erbyn hyn, wedi aeddfedu i fod tipyn fwy hyderus nac o'r blaen. Teimlai Llŷr yn annifyr yn ei gwmni, ond ni fyddai byth yn cyfaddef hynny.

Rhyw nos Wener, pan oedd bechgyn y dref yn ymgynnull yn y Bedol Arian, dyma Llŷr yn dechrau poeni Guto.

"Ti wedi dod yn ddyn o'r diwedd te Gut,' dechrau meddwl dros dy hunan, dechrau bod yn FI fawr ah?" Chwerthinodd yn uchel er mwyn denu sylw ei gyd yfwyr.

"Gwrandwch bois, mae Gut yn dechrau dangos ei ddannedd o'r diwedd. Pawb i fihafio nawr," bloeddiodd dros y bar. Ond tra roedd y ddau yn nhŷ bach y dafarn, rhoddodd Llŷr bwt galed i frest ei ffrind a sibrydodd yn ffyrnig i'w wyneb.

"Gwranda'n astud Gut, achos dim ond un waith yn unig wi'n mynd i ddweud hyn. Paid ti â meddwl dy fod yn mynd i fod yn well na fi mewn unrhyw ffordd gwd boi. Paid ti â mynd yn rhy fawr i dy 'sgidiau reit. Hy, s'dim rhyfedd bod ti wedi colli Angharad 'chwaith, bachan bach wyt ti wedi bod erioed ynte fe?" dywedodd yn watwarus gan edrych i lawr ar Guto'n cau ei gopis.

Yr eiliad nesaf, roedd Llŷr ar ei hyd ar lawr caled y tŷ bach, a'i lygad dde yn gyflym gau. Cododd ar ei eistedd gan rwtio'i wyneb.

"Fe ddifaru di wneud 'na,' dywedodd yn ffyrnig. Man uffarn i, mae fy nhrwyn i'n ffycin gwaedu. S'neb, ti'n clywed, neb wedi 'neud hyn i fi o'r blaen. Cer mas o'r ffycin ffordd y cachwr."

Ceisiodd Llŷr atal y gwaed a oedd yn diferu'n ffrwd goch i lawr

67

ei grys. Ni allai wynebu'r bobl yn y lolfa a sleifiodd allan drwy ddrws cefn y dafarn ac i anhysbysrwydd y nos, fel ci â'i gynffon rhwng ei goesau. Roedd ei falchder wedi ei falu. Ar y llaw arall, teimlai Guto rhyw ewfforia, rhyw ysgafnder, rhyw falchder ei fod wedi rhoi Llŷr yn ei le o'r diwedd. Chwarddodd yn dawel wrth gofio gweld Llŷr ar deils y tŷ bach, a'i wyneb yn mynegi syrpreis ac anghrediniaeth, a gwell na dim, siom.

Ond ar ôl i Guto gyrraedd adref ac ymdawelu, taenodd rhyw deimlad o ofn ac anesmwythder drosto. Gwyddai'n iawn na fyddai Llŷr yn maddau iddo, byth. Byddai'n rhaid iddo fod yn ofalus a chadw allan o'i ffordd o hyn ymlaen yn enwedig pan fyddai ar ei ben ei hunan.

Doedd dim croeso i Guto yn y Bedol Arian wedi'r noson honno. Roedd Llŷr yn amlwg wedi rhaffo rhyw gelwydd amdano a phawb o'r cydyfwyr wedi'i llyncu ac yn glynu wrth ei arwr. A chan nad oedd croeso i Guto yn y dafarn bellach, treuliai ei benwythnosau o hynny ymlaen adref gyda'i fam a photel o Budweiser o flaen y bocs. Doedd fawr o ddim ar y teledu y noson oer honno, a bu bron iddo fynd i'w wely'n gynnar, ond penderfynodd wylio ffeinal y peldroed pan ganodd y ffôn. Cafodd y neges fel un o hen ffrindiau Llŷr, fod hwnnw wedi ei ladd mewn damwain car ar y ffordd adref o'r dafarn ac Angharad yn ddifrifol wael yn yr ysbyty gydag anafiadau i'w phen a'i hwyneb. Mae'n debyg fod Llŷr wedi yfed gormod ac i'w gar daro derwen fawr wrth ochr y ffordd i'w gartref. Bu farw cyn cyrraedd yr ysbyty. Ni allai Guto gredu'r peth i Llŷrr ddiflannu yn llwyr o'i fywyd, fel hyn. Teimlai'n hynod annifyr ac yn isel ei ysbryd. Er nad oedd e

68

wedi siarad â'i hen ffrind ers misoedd bellach, nid oedd am y byd yn dymuno niwed iddo ef a'i wejen.

Ar ôl nosweithiau di- gwsg, a chyda'i fam yn ei annog, penderfynodd fynd i'r angladd .

Ond bu bron iddo redeg allan o'r capel pan welodd yr arch. Yna, daeth ato'i hun a cheisio ymdopi â'r sefyllfa. Cerddodd y tu ôl i'r teulu i'r fynwent y tu allan i'r capel a safodd yn barchus ar y mwswg trwchus gyda'r galarwyr eraill. Roedd hi'n gythreulig o oer, y cymylau llwyd yn addo eira cyn nosi. Ac yna, wrth i'r galarwyr ganu ar lan y bedd, dechreuodd y plu eira ddawnsio rywsut –rywsut o'i hamgylch, mor oer a distaw ac anghroesawgar â'r bedd newydd dorri o'u blaen. Fesul un, aeth y galarwyr adref. Safodd Guto'n llonydd ar lan y bedd yn gwylio'r dyn a'r JCB yn gorchuddio'r arch ac yn ei wahanu oddi wrth ei hen ffrind am byth, heb iddo gael yr un cyfle i ymddiheuro, nac i ofyn am faddeuant, na chael y cyfle i adnewyddu'r cyfeillgarwch a fu rhyngddynt am flynyddoedd maith. Edrychai Guto bron fel dyn eira, gyda'i wallt tywyll a'i got lwyd wedi eu brithio gyda'r tameidiau gwyn oerllyd.

"Cer adref Guto bach. S'dim byd alli di ei wneud yma," dywedodd y torrwr beddau'n garedig cyn ymadael â'r fynwent. Ond sefyll yn yr un fan a wnaeth Guto. A dyna a wnaeth am amser – hyd nes iddo sylweddoli ei bod wedi nosi. Tynnodd hances o ddyfnder ei got fawr, ac ar ôl sychu ei lygaid a'i ruddiau, trodd ac aeth at ei gar y tu allan i'r glwyd, gyda'r eira'n gyflym guddio ôl ei draed.

"Ble 'wyt ti wedi bod Guto?" gofynnodd ei fam yn bryderus pan gyrhaeddodd adref. "Mae bron yn chwech o'r gloch a we ni'n gofidio amdanat ti a'r car yn yr eira 'ma. Dere i gael tamaid o swper, ti'n edrych bron â sythu. Glywais i heddi fyd fod Angharad 'di symud i Ysbyty Treforys o achos yr anafiadau i'w phen a bydd rhaid iddi gael llawdriniaeth i'w hwyneb druan."

Eisteddodd Guto'n dawel yn ei got o flaen tanllwyth o dân, gyda'r eira'n llithro'n ddistaw ac yn dadlaith yn byllau bach o amgylch ei gadair.

"Dere â hanes yr angladd i fi te. A wedd llawer 'na? O, a chyn dy fod di'n dachre, ma' sawl galwad ffôn wedi bod heno fyd," dywedodd ei fam o'r gegin.

"Pwy we' ar y ffôn de?" gofynnodd Guto heb lawer o ddiddordeb.

"O'r hen alwadau 'na ti'n gwybod. Bob tro we ni'n ateb we' tawelwch yr ochr draw. Ateb di tro nesa' a rho lond pen iddyn nhw. Blydi niwsans."

Dihunodd Guto i swn y ffôn yn canu am un o'r gloch y bore. Rhedodd yn ysgafn droed i'r gegin i'w ateb gan obeithio nad oedd y swn wedi dihuno'i fam.

"Gut 'achan. Ti wedi cyrraedd adref o'r diwedd te," dywedodd y llais.

"Pwy sy'n siarad?" gofynnodd Guto'n flinedig.

"So ti'n 'nabod fi heno? Cer i'r Bedol Arian a dere â pheint o lager i fi a whisky chaser 'fyd i fi cael twymo'r bola. Dwi'n teimlo'n gythraul oer yn y twll din lle 'ma."

Syllodd Guto'n syn ar y ffôn cyn ei osod yn wyllt yn ôl yn ei le fel petai'r teclyn wedi llosgi ei fysedd. Dwi'n dychmygu pethe', meddyliodd. Ffrindiau Llŷr sy'n chwarae jôc arna i. Wnai ddim ateb y tro nesa.' Ond cyn iddo gyrraedd y grisiau, dyma'r ffôn yn ail ganu. Cododd Guto'r teclyn yn betrus i'w glust.

"Hey Gut 'achan, paid â rhoi'r ffôn i lawr ar dy hen ffrind 'to. Dere draw i gadw cwmni i fi. Dwi'n unig. Mae'r lle yn gyfyng iawn, ond we ni arfer bod yn ffrindiau agos. Rhaid watsho'r tinau rhag y ffycin ysgyrion cofia. Dere draw Gut, plis, dere draw."

Cyrhaeddodd Guto ei wely, ei feddwl fel nyth nadredd. A dyma fe'n gwneud rhywbeth nad oedd wedi ei wneud ers ei fod yn blentyn – dyma fe'n adrodd Gweddi'r Arglwydd.

Am dri o'r gloch, dyma'r ffôn yn canu eto. Gydag arswyd yn treuddio drwyddo, gafaelodd yn y ffôn, ei galon yn curo'n gyflym ac yn boenus yn ei fynwes.

"Ble wyt ti'r ffycer? Dwi bron â llwgu. Ffycin hell, os na allai ddibynnu ar hen ffrind i'm helpu, mae ar ben arna i,' meddai'r llais yn wyllt ac yna'n fwy addfwyn ' Rwy'n unig Gut, plis dere draw."

Gyda llaw grynedig, dyma Guto'n gwasgu un, pedwar, saith, un a dyma llais yn dweud wrtho pa rif oedd wedi ei alw. Bron iddo syrthio yn yr unfan. Teimlai fel petai wedi ei fwrw gan fwyell. Cydiodd yn ei got a rhedodd allan i'w gar. Ni arhosodd i wres y ffan ddadlaith ei ffenest flaen farugog cyn dechrau'r siwrnai. Teithiodd yn hanner gwyllt ar hyd yr heol nes cyrraedd y fynwent ar gyrion y dref. Cerddodd drwy'r eira trwchus tuag at y bedd. Syrthiodd ar ei liniau a chyda nerth annaturiol, annaearol bron, dyma fe'n dechrau ceibio o dan y trwch eira a oedd wedi gorchuddio'r beddau fel mantell fyglyd wen. Gafaelodd yn yr hyn a oedd yn chwilio amdano. Rhaid bod ei ffôn symudol wedi syrthio o'i boced i'r pridd meddal ffres wrth iddo dynnu ei hances a'i orchuddio gan yr eira. Rhedodd drwy'r fynwent, gan ddal ei ffôn i'r awyr gyda'i ddwy law, yn gweiddi ac yn 'sgrechian fel dyn o'i go. Cyrhaeddodd ei gar ac eisteddodd yn llonydd am eiliad. Taniodd yr injan, nes i'r swn ei gysuro.

71

"Chaiff y diawl 'na ddim gafael arna' i to," dywedodd yn uchel, ei anadl yn pwffian cymylau bach gwyn o'i flaen.

Gyrrodd ei gar ar hyd yr heol lithrig. Roedd hi'n dechrau gwawrio a theimlodd rhyw iachad, rhyw ryddhad yn yr addewid o ddiwrnod arall.

Penderfynodd ddechrau bywyd o'r newydd, bywyd braf heb fod o dan ddylanwad Llŷr dim mwy, a heb orfod byw o dan ei gysgod na'i fygythiadau, dim rhagor. Dechreuodd chwibanu.

"Twll dy din di Llŷr; a ti Angharad," gweiddodd yn uchel a dechreuodd chwerthin yn afreolus.

"Gwasg y brêc Gut," meddai llais o sedd gefn y car.

Edrychodd Guto yn wyllt yn ei ddrych a gwelodd Llŷr yn eistedd y tu ôl iddo.

"Does dim dihangid wrtha i gwd boi."

Yn ei wylltineb, gwasgodd Guto'r brêc a llithrodd y car yn afreolus oddi ar yr heol a syrthio'n ddwmbwr ddambar i lawr dros y dibyn cyn dod i orwedd yn wenfflam ar lawr y cwm.

72

Lliwiau

David Jones

Pan fydd gwyrdd y goedwig yn cochi gyda'r haul,
A melyn hydre'r felin ddŵr yn gymysg efo'r dail.
Pan fydd gwyn yr eira ar ochr Dal-y-Llyn,
A'r awyr oer yng Nghorris yn canu dros y glyn,

Pan fydd niwl Machynlleth yn cuddio Bro Glyndŵr,
A brithyll golau'r Dyfi yn neidio dros y dŵr.
Pan fydd llwyd y llechu yn ddu ymhlith y cwm,
A phiws y grug ar Idris yn gorwedd yno'n drwm.

Pan fydd llif y Mawddach yn torri sail y waun,
A thywod aur y Bermo yn gynnes fel y rhain.
Pan fydd lliwiau'r enfys yn gostwng fel y llu,
Daw llygaid glas y Dderwenlas i wenu arna' i.

Careful, She's a Fainter

Kelly Fitzgerald

"It's on the side! It's on the side! It's on the side!" These four
words course through my veins as I lay on the court. A thought in
my head – pounding, exclaiming, shouting, sobbing – my young
mind grasps the gravity of the situation, but cannot translate.
These four words travel up my esophagus, past my coated, ruby
uvula and hurtle over my teeth to escape.

"It's on the side! It's on the side!" I don't know what this means,
but they're the only words my traumatized mind can find; there's
too much pain. Like a wounded soldier who loses a leg but still
feels it there, I feel my arm where it's supposed to be, but see a new
arm dangling in front, as if I've grown a third. I don't know my
shoulder has dislocated. I don't know the technical terms, that my
ligaments and muscles have stretched, that tissues are torn and the
head of the humerus has slipped from the gleno-humeral joint in an
anterior dislocation, making my shoulder protrude forward in a

74

wrong way. All I know is it's on the side. It's on the side.

*   *   *

Female voices chatter in the distance, but I can't catch what they're saying. I try to open my eyes. I fail – there's only blackness. I can feel my body's presence, but cannot move. My limbs are heavy, as if gravity no longer exists and they're fighting to reach the floor. Someone moans nearby, eliciting a domino effect of moans, like a yawn. Another voice cries. Is something wrong? Someone needs to help! I try to open my eyes, but still cannot. Soon I become aware of my hands and that they're being held; I can't see the people, but sense them. I hear their muffled whispers and confirm that my parents are here beside me. I try to speak, but can emit no sound.

The smell finally wakes me. Worse than the skunk's spray I couldn't wash from my hair for a week, the stench of sterilized equipment turns my stomach. My eyes open and I glance to my side, where I assume my mother will be. She is and she smiles softly.

"How ya feeling?"

Like crap, like shit, like someone pummeled the life out of my lungs.

"Ok."

"Can I get you anything?"

I hesitate, honestly wondering whether anything I ask for could actually improve my situation. *A time machine to warp me six months from now when I'm all healed? Better yet, some new arms and industrial-strength shoulders to make sure they never detach again?*

"Underwear," I finally say, and she laughs.

"I can take care of that."

She pulls out the small bag I'd packed for the overnight stay and scrounges around. When she's found them she delicately folds down the blanket and sheet that are covering me, as if the pain has transferred from my shoulders to my toes. I slip my feet out and she helps me lift them slightly, threading each leg through the holes. *Wow. I'm seventeen, a senior in high school, but my mom is putting on my underwear. That's Fantastic.*

She doesn't seem the least bit uncomfortable and completes the job quickly and smoothly. *Who knew such a small piece of fabric could restore so much comfort and normalcy?*

"Socks, too?" she asks.

"Why not."

As soon as I'm dressed, a nurse flutters into the room as if on cue.

"Oh, great. Now that you're awake we can take you on a little walk!"

I want to smack the smile off her face. I don't have the energy for it, but I'm hoping Mom will receive my telepathic message and do it herself. Instead, she looks over and gives me that knowing, 'we've done this before, you know you don't have a choice' look. I think back to my first shoulder surgery – when the right arm was the one popping out, before the left – and know she's right. The nurse won't stop pestering me until I get up, act like I'm going to walk and then puke and faint to prove it was a bad idea.

"All right, but be careful, she's a fainter," Mom says, as she stands to help hoist my back from its downward position on the bed. The nurse moves over to help; she doesn't know my mom's freakishly strong. With their assistance, I'm surprised to find myself in a sitting position. Mom rounds the bed and prepares to take my right side as the nurse waits for my left.

"Easy does it," the nurse says. I swing my legs over so they're dangling off the edge of the bed. *I'm 5'10" and my feet still don't touch the floor. That can't be very safe.*

"Ok," I say, and slowly slip my body from the mattress and rest my feet on the floor. I am standing.

Before I ask, my mom maneuvers the yolk-colored kidney-shaped puke dish into sight and I let go. No hesitation, no time to think, it just comes – only because of pre-surgery fasting, I haven't had anything to eat in almost twenty hours, so there's not much result.

"She doesn't do well with anesthesia, either," my mom says, as she pulls Kleenex from her pocket to wipe my mouth. *She's my personal pit crew.*

"Ok, now that that's out of your system, how about we try a few steps?" the nurse says. I look over at my mom. *I can't believe she's going for more!*

"Whatever you say."

I take two steps and the blackness attacks. My head fills and the tingling reaches my eyes quickly. I can see the bathroom door in front of me, but it's diminishing fast. The darkness begins on all sides, a complete hollow circle, but converges quickly until there's no color left.

"She's going down, she's going down," I hear my mom say. *I told you so.*

I refocus quickly because I didn't entirely pass out; I never seem to make it the whole way there. One second I can see, the next the blackness takes over and I can only hear, but it ends there. The lightheadedness takes me down and one way or another sight gets restored.

Somehow they've sat me in a chair, and are both crouched down to my level. Once I'm lucid and have gained control again, my mom leaves to grab water from the bathroom sink. She fills a small paper cup and wets a washcloth to put on my forehead and neck.

"Just take it easy, take it really slow. We don't need to go anywhere." I don't think I smile outwardly, but it's pretty funny that my mom is taking control and contradicting the nurse's plans. *We'll show them!*

"Why don't I leave you two – it looks like you have everything under control. I have to check on a few other patients, but I'll be back soon with your lunch. That may help some." *Yeah, help turn my dry heaves into solid, multi-colored puke. Looking forward to it.*

After we've been sitting awhile I think I'm ready to move again – or at least try.

"Well, since we're this close to the bathroom, I might as well take advantage. There's no telling how long till we get this far again."

"Good point." Mom tosses the washcloth in the sink and the cup in the wastebasket before coming over to stabilize my stand. This time we have a bit more success and I make it about five shuffled steps to the toilet. *Thank goodness they make these hospital rooms so frickin' small!*

The uneasiness plummets to my gut again and I dive for the bowl as my mom holds onto my good arm and stops me from crashing into the linoleum. *And thank the Lord for whoever had the bright idea to leave the toilet seat cover UP!*

"Well, that was fun." I grab the Kleenex from her outstretched hand.

"You're doing well, honey. This is the worst part, it'll be over soon." Her voice is solid, unwavering, but I remember how much she hated this process the last time. And here we are again.

"You do what you have to do, but I'll be right outside. Just call if you need anything."

"Thanks, Mom." She leaves the tiny bathroom and closes the door, but not hard enough so that it clicks, giving me the privacy and independence I crave, but allowing the smallest of cracks so she can come to the rescue if needed.

After maneuvering my clothes with one hand, I sit down and revel in the fact that this time my right arm wasn't operated on, so it's free to do what needs to be done. *Much easier!* Of course, this delight is quickly struck down. Like many bathrooms, the toilet paper holder is on the left of the toilet. I can't bear the thought of moving any more than I have to, let alone rotating my entire torso to lean over my injured half and break off a few sheets of paper. *Any alternatives? Nope, the Kleenex and paper towels are both too far away. Brilliant.*

"Mom?"

Unbelievably, we make it back to the bed in one piece and without having to whip out the kidney-shaped devil. I sit on the bed and celebrate our recent success.

"Maybe you should have a little more water," she says and moves to get more.

"Uugh," is the only sound I can register. I don't really like water and she knows it.

"Or we could wait until they bring some juice or something with lunch."

"Better plan," I say, and she smiles. She gets me situated back on the bed and pulls down the covers and moves the pillows behind my head so I can see better. She also positions a smaller pillow securely under my injured arm so I don't have the added worry of unforeseen movement and pain.

"That good?"

"Yep."

We hear footsteps enter the room and both turn to see who's coming around the curtain. I'm certain I have my first visitor, but it's Dr Fix-it – not the type of visitor I was expecting.

"How's my patient doing?"

Well, I can't stop puking, my mom has to dress me like a two-year-old and so far I'm not really sure if I have both arms anymore, since I can't feel one. But other than that I'm superb.

"Fine."

"How does the shoulder feel?"

Like a colony of retired motor-home drivers have chosen my chest for their new abode.

"Like a ton of bricks." (I decide he'll respond better to this analogy.)

"Well, that's normal. We packed a lot of bandages and pads on there to keep it tight. Don't worry. In fact, you can move it around a bit, loosen it up." He starts to makes these wide, loopy gestures, as if I've had surgery to replace my bones with a slinky and would like to test it out. I don't think my face hides the fact I think he's insane. I never was a good liar.

"No thanks."

"Well, maybe a little later. You don't want it to get too stiff and tight."

Interesting. I thought that was the point. Wasn't I a bit too loosy-goosey before, with my joints fallin' out of place?

"Ok."

"Good, good. Well, I just wanted to come in, make sure

everything was going ok and tell you that the surgery went wonderfully, just as planned. Follow these recovery procedures (he hands my mother some pamphlets) and everything should be as good as new." He doesn't mention the two months of complete immobilization and three or four additional months of intense physical therapy just to get it up and working again…

"Sounds good, thank you Doctor." My mom gets up to shake his hand. "When do we need to schedule a follow-up appointment?"

"Oh, I'd say three or four weeks. The stitches are internal this time and will dissolve, but I'll take a look in about a month or so and make sure she's healing properly. Just call my office and set up an appointment."

"Ok. Thanks again."

"No problem." Dr Fix-it strides out of the room.

*   *   *

We both make it through the night. Sleep would have been nice, considering the day in bed was exhausting: I had monotone meals to enjoy, more quality time to spend with the kidney-shaped dish – which usually happened after I had a friend visit, because the increased talking was a little too much action for my stomach to take – a lovely gift of un-solidified Jell-O to appreciate (which I did so by falling asleep as my friends explained their cooking mishap) and a couple more lovely 'walks' to keep me busy.

Yet through the night, nurses kept coming into the room, waking us on the hour. There was always something to check, my pulse to take and of course my morphine drip to refill – although I didn't mind that too much. By the time morning came we were even more worn-out.

"Your mom's finishing up some paperwork and then you'll be set to go home," the nurse says. She un-collapses a wheel-chair and sets my overnight bag on its seat.

"All set." My mom is back and looking wary. "I grabbed an extra one of these, just in case." *Ah, my buddy the kidney-dish. Never leave home without it.*

They take their usual stations on each side of me, although this time I sit up on my own and maneuver myself off the bed – it's much easier, now that the initial surgery pain has worn off and I don't have to worry about the limited coverage of hospital gowns. (My mom had dressed me again this morning in my comfiest pajama pants and a button-up shirt that we deftly changed into without any lifting of the arm.)

I sit in the wheelchair and we are off. Sensing the motion sickness immediately, I rest my good elbow on my knee and my head in that palm. Mom pushes faster, knowing it would be better to get the journey over quicker.

"Wait here," she says, as she jogs into the parking lot and pulls up the car. Opening the passenger door, she helps me into the seat, tucks in my limbs and clothes and shuts the door.

"Ready?"

"Yeah, just get there fast."

The thought of the car moving is enough to make me reach for the dish – which mom has already placed on my lap. "Thanks." I ride the entire thirty-five minute drive with my right arm resting on the dashboard and my head resting on that arm. There is no other way to fight the sickness, or the pain.

"We're home."

I pry my head from the dash and look up. Yes we are. There in the driveway, when the garage door is lifted, is my little brother. His hands are resting on a folding chair, positioned in the center of the garage.

"We have the chairs all set. No worries this time, take it as slow as you want."

The first time I had surgery, we didn't realize how dizzy and weak I would be. When I had gotten out of the car and entered the house, there was no way I could make it to the steps, up the stairs, and through the living room to the recliner. It was just too far. So this time they have chairs waiting for me, positioned every twenty feet or so.

My mom parks the car and comes over to my side, stabilizing me as I get out, just like in the hospital. This time I have a new audience though. My brother stands there, his eyes wide and full.

"You ok?"

"Yeah, just a little tired." *I hope you never have to feel like this.*

My mom and I walk slowly into the garage and sit down. Chair one, accomplished. We wait.

"Ok, I'm ready to go again." My brother holds the door to the house. Mom lets me walk through first, but never lets go of my right elbow. There's another chair waiting for me in the foyer. I don't feel woozy this time, and know I can make it all the way to the stairs, but I catch my brother's eye and decide to defuse the moment by sitting down. No need to rush.

We make our way like this, slowly, taking about twenty minutes to finally reach our target: the upstairs recliner. On the wall, at the top of the stairs, is a computer-printed and colored sign that says, "Get Well Soon!"

"You do that?" I look at my brother. He nods, with a sheepish grin. "Thanks, buddy!"

"No problem."

There's a pillow and blanket laid out next to the recliner, plus a TV-tray with *People* magazine, a glass of apple juice and the remote control.

"Oh, Dad called and asked if you want anything special for dinner. He'll pick it up on the way home."

"How about Carbone's. Pepperoni and pineapple?"

"Yeah!" He rushes off to make the call, apparently pleased with my choice.

"Uugh, I feel so gross. I wish I could take a shower." I know I can't actually shower for a couple days, not until the bandages can be removed.

"If you're up to it, I can shampoo your hair. That'll make you feel better. We'll sit you right up to the sink, on the high stool," Mom says.

"Yeah, that'd be great."

"Want to do it now or later?"

"Now, for sure." She pushes the recliner leg down with her foot and helps hoist me out of the chair. Once again, like a seeing-eye dog, she leads me where I need to go, this time to the kitchen.

"You know, all this love and attention and getting waited on is pretty nice! I should get hurt more often. This surgery thing isn't that…"

"She's going down, she's going down!"

Deer Hunting

Bethany Pope

Muscles expand and contract
Fluid movement underneath brown fur
The dark, bright-liquid coal of an eye
Glimpsed between leaves
Caught in the last fading rays
Of the red, dying sun

The buck bounding through forest
Surrounded by leaves
Drenched in green water
That falls in pearls
From the limbs of the trees

Dancing past the silent cottage
Past the open window

Lit with candlelight
Open like an eye
Facing the darkness

*   *   *

She raises her fingers to her face
And feels the tacky, spreading blood
She looks out, curious,
From a black curtain of hair
That lies in thick coils
Around the base of her neck

His shoulders glide and dance
Beneath a thin patina of skin
Like the haunches of a lynx
Sighting a bird as it bathes in the river

He circles and darts,
Sinuous, around her
His hair spreading in a hood
Around his head

She stands still
Illuminated,
Transfixed by candlelight
Caught by the glare
Of an artificial sun

*   *   *

Muscles leap and contract
Beneath soft, brown fur
As the darkness expands
And covers the world

The dark gleam of an eye
Reflecting pale stars
Caught in the crosshairs
Of a loaded gun

The Emerald Dragon

Nadine Fry

Thomas couldn't sleep. He'd tossed and turned, pulled the covers right up to his chin, and then pushed them on the floor when he got too hot. Then he was too cold, and pulled them back on again.

He'd counted sheep and the glow-in-the-dark stars on his ceiling. He'd thought of all the boys' and girls' names in the alphabet, from Albert to Zebediah to Bob and Yasmina, but still he could not sleep.

So Thomas got up from bed and pulled on his fleecy dressing gown, wrapping it snugly around him. He walked over to his window and sat down on the sill, tucking his legs underneath him.

The moon was only a thin smile in the navy-blue sky, and only one or two stars peeped out from behind drifting clouds. He narrowed his eyes, trying to make out the shapes of the trees in the field. It was a very dark night.

Thomas' eyes started to ache, so he pressed his forehead against the cool pane of glass and closed them. He'd only been resting them a minute or two when a flash of light lit up the inside of his eyelids, making the tiny veins stand out like little roads on a map. He opened his eyes quickly, but all was still and black. He had his nose pushed up against the glass when he heard a tremendous BUMP!

Thomas opened his bedroom window, and pushed it as wide as it would go. When he was sure the rusty squeal hadn't woken his Mum or Dad, he leaned out as far as he could, craning his neck toward the roof.

All was silent. A cloud hid the moon. Thomas shivered. He waited for what seemed like an eternity, then finally the cloud passed and Thomas could just about make out a big, no, an ENORMOUS, shadowy shape on the roof. And with a horrendous noise that sounded like very long, sharp nails being dragged down a blackboard, the shape started to slide down the roof toward him.

Thomas closed his eyelids tightly and clutched the window frame with all his strength, his knees knocking together under his dressing gown. A loud swooshing sound filled the still air and a strange murky smell drifted up his nostrils. It smelt of burning leaves and peppermint. When Thomas opened them, a huge cloud of green smoke surrounded him. Looking up, he found himself staring into a gigantic pair of emerald-green eyes as big as dustbin lids. Scales like big shiny leaves covered an enormous body. Thomas felt hot, smoky breath on his face as a wide mouth opened to show rows of shining, silver teeth.

The swooshing noise started again, and hovering a few inches from Thomas' face was a magnificent, green dragon. Now that Thomas could see what it was, he wasn't scared at all, not one tiny bit. The dragon grinned at Thomas and winked one of his glittering emerald eyes. Thomas climbed out of his window and with bare feet, stepped on to the dragon's scaly body. Wings as big as airplanes started to flap and when Thomas was seated comfortably, the dragon took off at high speed.

They hovered over his house far below. Over dark hills and fields they flew, soaring above forests of trees, shadowy rivers and tumbling waterfalls. They flew over great black oceans, where dolphins somersaulted over foaming waves. And when the sun rose like a giant orange, they flew over lands Thomas had never seen before. Purple mountaintops sparkled with silver snow and huge lakes shimmered with gold and sapphire fish.

They swooped low over fields of tall, pink grasses that smelled of strawberries and cream, and trees whose branches dripped with strange fruit that glimmered and changed colours in the sun.

All day they flew, the dragon's powerful wings dipping and gliding, making Thomas' stomach somersault; his heart pounded and thumped, as the wind stole his laughter.

When the sun set and a ruby-red moon rose in the darkening sky, Thomas saw familiar fields and hills. And when he spotted his house, his eyes felt heavy with sleep. The emerald dragon hovered in front of Thomas' bedroom window, and as Thomas climbed in and waved goodbye, the dragon winked his glittering eye and disappeared into the night.

Thomas wearily climbed into bed and was asleep before his head hit the pillow, the scent of burned leaves and peppermint still in his hair.

Lost

Ansley Moon

Shock treatments, they decided
would cure her. After all, a woman
had a house to take care of. She
could not stay in bed all day
mourning her dead husband.
So three nurses strapped her
to a bed. One looked on
with a watchful eye, as another
dipped his dirty finger in the clear
gel before they applied the wires
one by one. She writhed and shook
in pain as the energy pulsated
through her tiny body.
Each zap was a memory
forgotten, a tender kiss,

a fragile gesture lost.
Of her husband, lover,
and father of her children.

The Last Oasis

Sharon Tregenza

Sindy settled back in her seat to watch for camels. As the silver Toyota Land Cruiser left Dubai, the early morning heat shimmered above the concrete buildings and the spire of a dun-coloured mosque. She began to sing, "I wanna be loved by you, by you, and nobody else but you, coo coo cachew," clicking the nails of her left hand on the window glass in rhythm. Dan glared at her.

"I don't know why I agreed to this," he said. "You can't even swim. I could've played golf today."

"I thought it would be nice for a change. You know, just the two of us." Sindy rummaged in her handbag, sighed, and tumbled the contents into her lap. Picking up the compact mirror and a tube of lipstick, she made an 'O' shape with her mouth, and with the slow concentration of a child, smeared her lips with Fuchsia Red. When she slipped a cigarette from the packet, Dan glared at her again.

"Don't light that," he snapped. "I don't want you stinking out

93

this new car with your filthy smoke." Sindy put the cigarette back in the packet.

The big four-wheel-drive sped on. The roads, clear and straight, were lined for miles with wire and wooden stake fences to keep the camels from wandering on to them.

"One, two, Ooh and a baby one, that's two and a half," Sindy said. She wriggled her plump body against the seat belt to reach the car radio. The sudden blast of music made them both jump. Dan snapped the radio off again.

"You said you wanted to try Wadi bashing," he snarled, "so here we are, bloody Wadi bashing." He revved the car and slammed it into overdrive. "Though, why the hell people want to motor through blistering heat and desert to find a patch of water is beyond me. I hope you enjoy it, because I won't." Sindy hunched her shoulders and stared down at her feet.

They drove through Fujairah, the car's air conditioning purring in the silence as they passed dozens of little stores – steel pans hung in glittering bunches and multi-coloured plastic bowls and buckets festooned the shop fronts. The air rippled with heat and the sky and the sea matched in a perfect jigsaw blue. The thin, tinny cry of the Muezzin echoed from a minaret. Sindy closed her eyes.

Her head snapped forward suddenly when the car screamed to a stop. A fat Arab woman, dressed in the voluminous black abaya, stood motionless in front of them. Dan shouted at her, swearing. Sindy watched the cords of veins knotting at his throat. The woman stood her ground and then turned to face them. Her eyes glittered black behind the leather mask worn over the top half of her face. Slowly, she extended her hand with the fingertips pressed together

94

in the contemptuous Arabic sign for wait! Enraged, Dan pressed his foot hard on the accelerator. With astonishing speed the woman lurched back from the road on to the sand. Dan laughed. Sindy put her head down, letting the wings of golden hair hide her burning face.

The landscape merged into the yellow, orange and bleached beige of swollen sand dunes and the heat danced its water patterns off the road. Sindy took out another cigarette, and then remembering, put it away again. They drove on through the stone-edged prettiness of Khor Fakkan. The blinding dazzle of the sun's path stretched over the blue Gulf of Oman.

"There are two small farmhouses around here somewhere." Dan's voice broke the silence. He snatched the map from the back seat and thrust it into her hand. The farms were easy to spot – two run-down houses surrounded by agricultural rubbish and desperate patches of green. Stringy chickens pecked indiscriminately, heads and legs flicking in comic unison. Between the farms, a rough track twisted its way to the mountains. Dan pulled off the road and on to the track with a squeal of tires. He pushed the gearstick into automatic four-wheel drive. The chickens scattered, squawking.

"Stop, Dan!" Sindy shouted. "Stop the car!" She fumbled with the door and jumped out. A searing blast of heat slammed in, forcing out the cool air. Dan swore. He watched his wife stumble in her high heels over to a small pile of rubbish. She returned holding a skinny kitten against her neck.

"Look, Dan," her eyes shone. "Isn't he sweet, the poor thing, he's starving."

Dan pursed his lips with distaste. "Put it back."

"But, Dan."

Sindy put her free arm on her hip and lisped in the wheedling tone that had entranced Dan many years ago.

"The little babba wanta Mamma and Dadda."

"Get rid of it," he hissed.

Sindy returned the mewling kitten. "Sorry, baby," she whispered, planting a scarlet kiss on its dry skull.

The track became harder to find as the car dragged over ever-bigger obstacles. Dan's hands whitened as he gripped the wheel. The gravel surface of the mountains, gleaming the muted shades of autumn, spread out before them as the heat and the day wore relentlessly on. A fat fly threw itself at the rear window with sticky insistence. They hadn't seen another car since they had left the road and Sindy wondered what would happen to them if they got lost. She frowned and closed her eyes.

"At last!" Dan said.

She woke to see a patch of green bamboo and then another. The Wadi – the riverbed. It cut a swathe through the harsh, slate gray rocks towering above them on either side. Dan smiled for the first time since they'd left home.

They heard the waterfall before they saw it. The four-wheel-drive stumbled through a shock of greenery and there it was, the sight and sound of the water, delicious, cool and sweet in the hard dust heat. Dan sat mesmerized, as the white foam crashed down through the red-brown rocks high above them. The sun, full upon it, turned the swift slide at the top into a stream of gold and silvered the whitening rush as it fell.

Hurriedly, Dan climbed over the boulders, up high to the source of the stream. Sindy tried to follow, but her shoes twisted and slipped on the smooth rocks. She pulled them off, making squealing noises when the heat burned her feet. The exertion made her sweat, and dark patches shadowed her dress under her arms. She looked to where Dan, high above her, lay stomach down, watching the water.

"Help me, Dan."

He sat up and shaded his eyes from the sun. Then slowly, deliberately, lay back down on the rock. Sindy clambered on, trying not to look to where the water streamed down to the pool below. She was two-thirds up when she fell, stumbling and slipping over the edge. The sound of the waterfall crashed in her ears as she clung to the rock face. There was a sharp pain in her knee. A fine spray dampened her hair and clothes. Sindy looked down and saw the pool far below, black and deep. A needle of fear pierced her once, and then again. She heard Dan's voice.

"Your hand," he shouted over the boom of water. "Give me your hand!" She looked dazedly at her free hand and realised she was still clutching her shoes.

"Drop them!" Dan's voice struggled for control. "Drop the bloody things!" They plummeted like birds shot in flight, into the darkness, the thud of the waterfall swallowing the sound as they hit.

But Sindy wasn't watching her shoes; she was watching Dan. His hand held hers – hard – his face so close that she could see the glitter of contempt in his eyes. She felt his hesitation.

Instinct told her not to speak, not to move. She stared dumbly up at him, trying to control the trembling of her body. The roar of water and singing heat rolled and twisted together over and over inside her head. Her knee hurt, but still she didn't move. Dan gave a small shudder and shouted, "Hold tight!"

97

As he pulled, she braced her feet against the slippery surface and with one movement was over and safe. She lay on a small plateau of rock, breathing heavily. The pink dress was wet and dirty; blood made thin red tracks across her calf. She sat up, rubbed at her knee with her finger and then touched the blood to her lips and the tip of her tongue.

"I'm going home now," she said.

"We're not going anywhere until I've had a long swim." Dan turned and headed away from her. She watched him as he discarded shorts and t-shirt, stripping down to his swimming costume. She watched as he poised his slim, tanned body at the edge of the green pool and as he did a perfect dive into the water. Then Sindy stood up.

The pedals burned her bare feet. "Ouch," she said. As she drove away, she thought she heard a shout, but it could have been the sound of the waterfall. For a long time she drove, keeping the mountains behind her. The car clung to the big boulders, crawling up and down and over them like a hard-backed beetle. Sindy turned the radio up loud and lit a cigarette. "It's not unusual to be loved by anyone," she sang. "It's not unusual to have fun with anyone."

When, at last, she reached the farms, the sparse trees around them were silhouettes, their arms black-green in the festering light. A sweet salt breeze blew in from the sea. Sindy stopped the car and got out.

"Here kitty, kitty," she called. "Here kitty, kitty."

Lady Eve

David Jones

I'm sorry to be missing you with every brand new day,
I wonder who'll be kissing you since your love went away.
Will Auld Lang Syne and summertime mean just the same to you,
Or will that blanket on the ground caress the morning dew?
Will Peggy Sue grow up to be the lady dressed in red,
Or will she wait to runaround in Grandma's feather bed?
Will Bacharach or Ramblin' Jack compose a song for you
To say that you're a lady in a world of misty blue?

Will everybody ask you why the sun ain't gonna shine?
Will old Jack Flash or Johnny Cash forget to walk the line?
If everybody's talking 'bout the free electric band,
Will John and Paul and George and all still want to hold your hand?
If Ruby came on Tuesday would Monday come behind?
Would Sunday morning come on down with Friday on my mind?

Will the Hotel California close its doors for evermore?
For the surfin' sound is homeward bound to the banks of the Ohio.

Will Graceland ever hear again another trilogy?
Will the Doobies ride the long train in perfect harmony?
Will Stevie call to say that you look wonderful tonight,
And how you make so many lives so beautiful and bright?
Will the Yellow River flow from the Black Hills to the sea?
Will red sails shine on the blue bayou and the green in Innisfree?
Would you believe it if I said I didn't mean to be unkind?
You're more than once a lady and were always on my mind.

Avalanches

Sandra Mackness

"If we're going for this, we really must put our money where our mouth is?"

"That's about it, babes. Any bright ideas?" Ben resumed his pacing, quite an achievement in that kitchen.

Amanda moved over to the sink. Water gushed into the kettle. "Tea or coffee?" she asked.

Ben frowned and pushed back a slick of fresh laundry so she could place two mugs on the worktop. "Tea, please. Maybe it'll help me think."

"Maybe," she said. She already knew what she was going to do.

*   *   *

Amanda concentrated on not spilling the contents of her teacup in her lap. In theory, she could put the cup and saucer on the floor, thus enabling her to clear a space on the coffee table. Auntie Beth's precarious piles of seed catalogues, spectacle cases, remote controls, pens and an open fruit gum packet were the obstacles. One false move could trigger a rainbow-coloured avalanche. Amanda decided against rearrangement. Thick, dark chocolate melted where her biscuit was touching her cup.

"It does seem like a good idea, darling. Simple, yet practical. And he thought it up … all on his own?"

Amanda winced. Juggling her teacup, she sucked her forefinger and bit into the crunchy Bath Oliver. "Yes, Auntie. All the credit must go to Ben."

"You have the skills. I've no reason to doubt your ability. Mind you, I've always thought you had a better brain than Ben. He can't be too bright if he's still not proposed to you."

Amanda laughed. "We have a … an understanding. We were hoping to form the business partnership first, then let the marriage thing happen … in its own time."

Her aunt shook her head, wisps of hair drifting like smoke. "You young folk. I can't really make you out."

"We're not that different," Amanda assured her. "It's just that we've changed the order of play."

"So, exactly how much money do you need?"

*   *   *

"That is so amazing, sweetheart. The old gir… I mean your auntie has offered to sell one of her precious knickknacks? She'd rather do that than loan you some cash?"

"Apparently. She said I'd be inheriting a lot of her furniture and stuff one day, anyway."

"What about the house?"

"Her late husband's son will inherit."

"Pity," said Ben. "Even so, that vase … what do you reckon it's worth?"

*　　*　　*

"Auntie Beth, Amanda and I are really thrilled at your generous offer. Hey, Beth, isn't it time I stopped calling you Auntie?"

Alone in her aunt's kitchen, Amanda cringed at Ben's gushing tone, but was consoled as she imagined him coping with crockery and biscuits. Ben detested disorder and, if anything, the table was even more pyramid-like than on her previous visit. Yet, despite Beth's unconcern about living in a muddle, her mind was an incisor. Amanda scalded the ground coffee, breathing in the rich aroma as she waited for the brew to settle in the pot.

"It's stunning," Ben was exclaiming as Amanda crossed the hallway.

Auntie Beth stood on the hearthrug, holding the priceless, yet monstrous old vase in front of her. Amanda had always detested its unlikely shade of baby-poo, not to mention the squat shape and the handles, so reminiscent of Prince Charles' ears. How could anything so unattractive be so valuable? It was stunning all right. She placed the tray on the floor and knelt to fill the cups.

"I know what you're thinking," Auntie Beth fixed her gaze upon Ben. "How can the woman find anything amongst all this muddle?"

"I like a home to have that lived-in quality," Ben smirked, looking in vain for a landing strip. He nudged aside a pool of embroidery silks and moved a spectacle case to part the clutter. His

103

excitement, almost palpable as he smelt the cash potential in the room, rattled his cup and saucer into a crash landing onto the glass-topped table. A fat paperback thudded to the carpet.

Auntie Beth, startled, took a step forward. One foot twisted and as she struggled to find her balance, the vase plummeted to the floor. It fell like the ball in a slow motion television replay.

. Ben lunged forward to catch it on its way down. After all, he was a rugby player. But the voluptuous settee cushions were disinclined to release him.

"Jesus Christ … is that my future down the tubes?" he snapped as the vase bounced on the carpet.

"Your future?" said Aunt Beth.

Ben's remark buzzed like an angry wasp inside Amanda's head as she scrambled up from the carpet to reach her aunt's side. The old lady had collapsed into her armchair. Her fingers pressed pale patches on her lips. Ben was on his knees, prising his fingers under the vase so he could cradle it in his palms, the better to check for damage.

"Just leave it, please."

Ben apparently did not hear.

"I said, just leave it."

Ben looked up, his face unravelling at something unmistakeable in Amanda's expression. Unnerved, he got to his feet, gesturing his uncertainty; he looked from one woman to the other. His lips tightened. He nodded and left the room. The sound of the front door banging hung like an exclamation mark in the air.

It was Auntie Beth's turn to comfort her niece, though it was difficult to tell whether her tears were from relief or distress. After Amanda wiped her eyes and blew her nose, she lifted her chin. "Thanks for not saying I told you so."

She returned home to find a note on the kitchen table.

Amanda, we can still make it happen. Please ring me. I'm just off to the florist's. We'll take Beth a huge bouquet and I'll grovel to the old girl. You were overwrought, babes. I quite understand. Back soon. Ben xxx

Amanda glanced at the crowded breakfast bar. Her mobile phone was half-buried under a pile of glossy magazines. She crumpled Ben's note into a ball – aimed it at the photo smiling from the cork message board. It struck his face between the eyes and bounced on to the floor.

When You Die

Ansley Moon

Rest assured,
I will attend
your funeral.
To make sure
they put you
in the ground.
I'll throw rocks,
instead of roses,
on your coffin.
Just to make sure
you can't breathe.
Or come back
to haunt us.
I'll stay after.
Until the soil
is smoothed.
And you
are really gone.

County Mayo

Sandra Mackness

The wine flowed at our engagement party, and Louise was flirting with my Mark. I found the mayonnaise, dipped a finger in, and glided over with some sausage rolls. Louise was giggling. I laid my hand affectionately on her scarlet silk shoulder.

"Did you tell Louise where we're going on honeymoon, darling? I asked.

"We're off to County Mayo," Mark smiled.

Keep

Sue Moss

Very early in the morning Grace wakes to the sound of her own heavy breathing. She coughs and pulls the thin sheets tightly under her chin. Through the gloom the clock radio shows five forty-five. Too early. She lies in bed till it's time to get up. When it is she dresses quickly and fills the kettle. The neighbours are preparing for their day. John's carrying something in a brown bag to the wheelie bin at the end of his path. Grace glances at her own bin, half hidden by a painted trellis provided by the site. Each caravan has one at the end of its path; it was a deciding factor when they chose this park. A decent sized plot with trellis fencing for privacy, and adequate parking facilities.

The ritual in the mornings is simple, as Grace never eats breakfast. It's not worth it – not for one. She makes tea and flicks on the TV. She swigs back her tablets and watches the news. When Jed was with her they'd have toast or a cake. Jed had a sweet tooth.

He loved a doughnut. She swallows the rest of her tea, watching the news with the sound off, and decides what to do with her day. It's hard to know what to do all the time. Mostly she walks to the shops for a paper, brings it home, reads the news and her stars, watches TV, and chats to neighbours. When Jed died she gave his car to Jeffrey. He never drove it, only to take it to a garage and sell it. She's pleased he got a good deal though. No sense it just sitting there at the end of the path. Just reminding her. Jeffrey drives a new car now, plenty of room for the children: three of them. Pictures of her grandchildren crowd every surface – baby photos through to group portraits at school and the boys playing sports with their dad, and the girl dressed up for a party. When John and Sonia pop in they always take trouble to enquire after the family, though they've never met. Sonia and John have one daughter living in Spain. Grace thinks it would be difficult to have your family so far away.

In the afternoon Sonia drops in to talk about the end of season's plans. Grace prefers not to discuss this but Sonia ploughs on. "We'll be staying at Julie's until New Year. It rarely drops below sixty-eight. Just right." She tells Grace they'll be booking into the Sol Y Sombre in Portugal for two months after that, until they're able to return to the site at the start of the new season. They've been doing it for years. Best thing they ever did was to sell that big old house and move here. They can travel all over in the winter. Gives them freedom, she says. Grace agrees, nods her head repeatedly. It nearly gives herself a headache, so she pops a pill once Sonia leaves.

Her plans involve Jeffrey, she's sure. She's not too worried about money, not really. They had some savings and gave money to their son from the sale of the house. Then Jed died before they'd been here six months. Jeffrey agreed it was right for his mother to stay on at the site. He knew how much his dad loved it here. She wasn't worried about the end of the season. Not really.

The next evening Sonia taps at the door. Grace was invited for supper, but has forgotten. Sonia stands smiling, beckoning with her hand, waving her in like a fussy parent, "Knew you'd forget. Come on, I've cooked a lovely bit of ham. John's putting cream in the mash. We've got wine. Come on." Laughing, she walks toward her own caravan, making a show of holding the wooden gate open for her guest to pass through.

"I'm starting to worry now, Gracie." John ladles the steaming mash onto her plate. Sonia's swallowing red wine and when she smiles, reveals a plum moustache. "I said, Gracie, I'm starting to worry." Grace is not keen on John's chosen nickname for her. She lets it go.

"Nothing to worry about, John. I'll be at Jeffrey's."

"I'm sure, but for four months love? That's quite a stint." He starts into his mash with purpose.

"John, Jeffrey's her son. It's up to them." Sonia refills their glasses.

"I'm not being rude, I'm just concerned."

Grace assures her friends she'll be fine. When the site closes for winter, Jeffrey will pick her up. He'll probably bring the children – although that might be a squeeze, all five of them with her luggage.

"He'll need to convert his garage, Gracie. Into a little granny flat for you." Grace isn't sure how serious John is, so changes the subject.

During the week that follows, the whole site prepares for its annual closure. The swimming pool and bar are locked and someone's covered the pool. Many couples have left and most dropped in to say 'bye,' and 'wish you well,' 'see you soon,' and 'have a lovely holiday.' Liz and Neil, a couple in their forties, are the site officers and always friendly. They sent beautiful flowers to Jed's funeral. They're concerned for Grace's welfare and call in several times during the final week to check all's well.

"A week Wednesday, Grace. Will Jeffrey be here to look after you?"

"Oh yes. Yes. Like I said. Whatever the date – you know, he'll be here."

"Well, that's good. I'll pop in before then."

It begins to rain as Grace waves goodbye. Liz scurries to her car, turns to smile, ducks in and drives away. When Jed died, Liz and Sonia took turns bringing food to the caravan every day. Swaying in with pies and cakes, home-baked pastries, they'd helped to steady the ship. That was John's expression. "Gracie, we're just here to steady the ship, keep things going." They behaved like members of her family. They moved into her life and she didn't mind. They were solid, not likely to bend if the wind blew up suddenly.

"Just be sure to tell Jeffrey when you want to leave."

"Liz, don't worry. It's all arranged."

Sonia once commented on Liz's anxiety, adding that she'd worry too if she thought it would do any good. "Does keep you thin though, worry." The women laughed.

Grace is fond of Liz. She remembers in the early days following Jed's death that she was in a muddle and nothing made sense and her tongue wouldn't work. She'd been with a group of neighbours at Sonia's where they were discussing the alarming case of the 'mad knife incident.' A man had gone on a rampage in the town, with knives he'd stolen from the kitchens where he worked. He'd been arrested while brandishing the stolen weapons at complete strangers. Thankfully, he was foreign. "Not a local person at all." Grace was relieved to inform the group that order was restored, as the foreigner had been incinerated in the police cells. Her neighbours collapsed helpless with laughter. Liz rescued her, said, "You mean incarcerated, Grace." She'd smiled lightly and that was that. Grace accepted the joke as her own and would revel in its retelling.

Late Tuesday morning, Grace leaves another message for Jeffrey. Just a quick one; she hasn't quite finished packing. She has the rest of the evening. Wednesday at eleven, she's told him. She hopes she's not the last to leave. At six Liz raps at the caravan door.

"Grace, you're still here!"

"Well, yes, I'll be off tomorrow though."

"Now, I insist you come over for supper."

"Oh, Liz , thank you. It's just.."

Food is out of the question. Grace feels sick, very deep down.

"I won't hear of it. If you're not at ours in twenty minutes, I'll be back."

On Wednesday afternoon, Grace's belongings are packed and ready to go. She sits among them in her spotless caravan. A light rain falls and there's a threat of thunder behind the trees at the edge of the site. Grace has packed her most precious pieces in a large red bag, which rests at her feet. She runs a finger along the framed photo jutting out at the top. She keeps the worry from her face by yawning, deeply and for too long. She watches clouds gathering behind the trees and hopes the thunder holds off.

Memorising Her Movements

Nicky Herriot

It's a long drive, but worth it. I'm following the road that winds
around the lake. It's a hot day, making it hard to concentrate, but
there are no cars ahead, so the driving is easy. I know where I'm
going as I've done this journey several times now. I check the rear
view mirror and see a blue Audi TT catching up. As I get to the
final straight, I slow down to let it overtake. I don't need any
disturbances today. I don't need them behind me. The car
disappears in a blast of noise. I take a minute to wonder if they're
going to the same car park, but I dismiss it. I pass the lake hotel and
take the last tight bend that tells me I only have a few miles to go.
My heart rate increases and I breathe slowly to calm myself. It is,
after all, about self-control. Checking my mirror again for traffic, I
indicate left and pull into the car-park.

There are a couple of cars, one of which is slowly moving
toward me, on its way out – which is good. There's an elderly

couple in it. Elderly people think they can talk to me. Don't they realise I have work to do? I don't have time to talk. I park at the far end, away from the gate. I don't need to look for the other car to know it's there. It will be there. Careful not to slam the door, I lock my car and take a few moments to breath deep again. I'm ready.

I pass through the gate and up through the woods. Once past the cottages, the path divides. This does not cause a problem; they will all lead me to the same area. Yet, it's all part of the test. I choose carefully. I take the track that leads me closest to the stream. She would have chosen this one. I walk carefully and quietly – no kicking stones or disturbing the undergrowth. She wants to know I have skill. She wants to know I care.

My heart beats faster as I pass the detour to the waterfall. I turn left and take the path away from the stream. I know where she will be. I know where she wants me to be. I find my place. I am ready.

*　　*　　*

I'm sitting against my tree, hugging my knees, tucked into the shadows. Watching.

Yesterday I couldn't see the water. They put picnic tables by the river. They were in my way. I couldn't see the rock anymore.

This place is new. More shadow. Much better. I can see her from here. I smell the damp earth beneath me – the leaves, the mould. This is wrong. I want to smell the water. I want to smell what she can smell.

But not yet.

I'm watching her so carefully, memorising her movements. Memorising everything she gives me. She sits on the bank, her feet

114

in the water. Her back is to me. But she knows I'm here. She is teasing me. I see her through the trees.

I taste the oily steam before I hear the train as it comes over the bridge. I stiffen, ready to move. I hate that train. It distracts her. It takes her attention away from me. She has followed it up to the station before.

Today she knows. She stays with me. She waves to the passengers. She is too friendly. She could come to harm because of her friendliness. She needs me to watch over her. She climbs onto the rock, and stretches out her legs. She is wearing my favourite shorts. For me. Her white legs are bright from lack of sun. She is still barefoot. They might think it's so she doesn't get her shoes wet. I know the truth. Her bare toes wiggle in the sunshine. She is telling me to come over.

But not yet.

There is no one on the path. They have followed the train up the hill.

She lies flat on our rock. She is telling me she wants me there. It's time.

I pick up my jacket and cut through the trees to her. To our rock.

She pretends not to notice me. She likes playing these games. She lies still. She wants me to speak first.

I choose my sentence carefully. She must know that I'm the one. The one who looks after her.

"You've walked a long way to get to our rock."

She looks up, startled.

She stares at me. She looks as if she doesn't know me. This is not in the rules. I feel the anger rise inside of me. I stay calm. I look up the hill, to the skyline, where the rooks are squawking on the wind.

She will know me.

115

The Elan Valley (Revisited)

David Jones

The sheep-shorn hills and barren peaks survey
The mirror lakes that feed the babbling brooks
That race away from deep kinetic stores.
The forlorn cries of orphaned lambs call out
To those of yore who once had lived
In solitude beneath the pebble shores.

The pinecones glisten as fragrant strands
Of heather moss and floss of airborne seed
Descend from mellow crystal haze.
The water simmers still as breezy banks
Of mountain thyme array the foot-worn path
That forms the linear trail of dark green maze.

She walks by the river in slender pose,
Her tender arms held out expectantly to
Welcome a long lost friend from a distant past.
Her soft white woollen drape that once was laid
Across the curvatures of several mountain ewes
Concealed her dwindling body mass where fate was cast.

She hums a Welsh lullaby that once we shared
Before the fatal fever left its mark and curse
Of premature loss for those she knew.
Though the valley looks the same with her laughter gone,
Seclusion darkens every ray of golden sun
As memories return to haunt the olden few.

My Son

Sharon Tregenza

He's gone,
        and grown,
                and gone my son –

Now who
    will make a dandelion necklace for his Mum?

Getting There

Jacqui Burns

I tried to shake the pins and needles from my legs but the area was too cramped. The selfish bastard in front of me had reclined his seat so far back I could see the open pores on the top of his head. I contemplated spilling my glass of Lambrusco over him but it seemed a waste of cheap wine.

Ben winked at me. He was looking terribly smug. "This is the life, Tash. This is why we work forty-five-hour weeks. Malaga, here we come." He drained his glass of lukewarm beer and winked again.

"Someone's looking pleased with himself." I couldn't help smiling. "I just wish we could have had seats next to each other," I said, motioning to the two small boys sitting next to me. It was okay for Ben; he had the mum and dad next to him. I lowered my voice and stretched across the aisle closer to Ben, "You'd think their parents might have separated so the boys wouldn't have been alone."

Ben nodded but he didn't seem unduly perturbed. I was worried that Jordan, the boy closest to me, was going to throw up any minute. He'd eaten a whole packet of Minstrels already and we'd only been on the plane half an hour. Not only that, but they fought every few seconds over the toys they had with them. One was this rubber Homer Simpson doll that had stretchy limbs. Earlier on they'd been tugging at his legs in opposite directions and Jordan's brother suddenly released his grip, sending Homer Simpson's underpants at full force into my chin. God, if ever there was an effective form of contraception, this had to be it: spending time in the company of two small, hyperactive boys in a space in which you couldn't swing a kitten, let alone a cat. I was beginning to see why the parents had chosen not to sit by them.

I could hear a rattle from the trolley behind me. Great, food at last. I'd been living on Tic-Tacs and apples for the last fortnight in the hope that I didn't disgrace myself on the beach. I was quite pleased as I'd lost half a stone. I'd treated myself to a white crocheted bikini and judging by Ben's jaw-dropping reaction when I tried it on in the flat, all my hard work was going to be worthwhile.

I'd pinned a lot on these two weeks in Malaga. Ben and I hardly had time for each other these days with us both being so busy at work. We flopped into bed at night with barely enough energy for anything other than a peck you give distant aunties at funerals. It was time we recaptured the fireworks in the bedroom. I'd even invested in a couple of sessions in the spray-tanning booth at the local salon. As Ben said when we were in the departure lounge, I had a better tan than those returning from a month in the Maldives.

"God, I'm starving," Ben said, looking back at the stewardess serving the passengers behind us. I noticed his gaze linger a bit longer than necessary on her bum encased in its tight grey pencil skirt. I scowled and Ben quickly turned away. If ever I owned an airline, I vowed I'd only employ stout, matronly stewardesses with blackheads and facial hair. I couldn't even make Ben jealous by flirting with the only steward on board, Oliver as his name tag revealed, as he looked as if he'd have trouble getting in to see a twelve certificate movie at the UCI.

The stewardess, Leah, handed trays over to the two urchins before serving me. "Enjoy your lunch," she said with crisp, lipsticked efficiency and then turned to Ben. He flushed as she leaned over, her white blouse gaping wide.

"Slut," I murmured, peeling the cardboard lid from my lunch. Jordan and his brother jerked their heads toward me. "Yum," I said, looking at the food. I tied hard to cover my disappointment. A minuscule piece of chicken in a white, gloopy sauce was served with reconstituted mash and a tablespoon portion of peas. There was certainly no danger of ruining my diet.

"Will you help me take the lid off? It's stuck," Jordan asked. "And Connor's."

"Sure," I said.

"Can you help me with mine?" Ben grinned.

"Get lost," I told him.

Dessert was a slippery piece of crème caramel and dry crackers and cheese.

"When's Jamie Oliver going to turn his attention to airlines, do you think?" Ben asked. Obviously nothing was going to dampen his mood, not even the rotten food. "Come on, cheer up. I'm going to order us champagne."

I didn't argue, especially when I saw Jordan opening a packet of Haribos. If he was going to puke, the least I could do was get so rat-arsed I wouldn't notice. I clipped the tray to the back of the seat in front and rummaged around for the in-flight magazine as we waited for Leah to return with the drinks. I was annoyed to discover I'd left my book on the bed at the flat. It was Jackie Collins's latest bonkfest – just the kind of reading I fancied for the long snoozy hours on the beach. There were only two articles to read in the magazine: one on the ruination of Prague due to its becoming the favourite destination of lager louts and the other giving tips on how to avoid deep vein thrombosis, alongside an advert for thick tangerine support stockings. The rest of the magazine was filled with price lists of the tragic gifts on board: weird looking teddies dressed in the captain's uniform and chunky gold watches and bracelets Del Boy would have had trouble shifting from his suitcase in Peckham market.

I swallowed the champagne in huge gulps and Ben ordered another. I was beginning to feel more relaxed. This was more like it. The bubbles tickled my nose and my limbs began to feel warm and heavy. I finally allowed myself to indulge in the holiday mood, and wasn't even bothered when I was re-introduced to Mr Open Pores as he slid his seat back and began snoring noisily. I crossed my legs and my denim skirt slipped up my tanned thighs. I opened my legs slightly, basking in Ben's appreciative glances.

I quickly looked down the aisle behind me. Why not, I thought. I shot Ben what I hoped was a seductive look and whispered, "I'm off to the loo. Do you need to go?" Ben said nothing, but his mouth gaped open in surprised pleasure. "Don't be too long," I added, trying to walk in a straight line despite the cramp in my ankles.

I was grateful to see the green 'Vacant' light flashing above the lavatory. I squeezed in, locking the door behind me. Looking in the mirror, I ran my fingers through my hair and applied a coat of lip-gloss. I peeked down at the stainless steel toilet seat and saw that it was wet with urine. Dark stains decorated the shiny toilet bowl. God, there was a horribly pungent smell in there, too. It wasn't the least bit romantic. More vile-high than mile-high. I turned round to look at the sink. The tiny tablet of soap had disintegrated, leaving slimy white smudges all over the place. Could I really hitch my bum up there? It was no bigger than a soup bowl. I was sure if I leaned against it the whole thing would come off the wall. Oh well, it was too late now. I could hear Ben's breathing outside before he tapped gently on the door.

I undid a couple of buttons on my blouse so that it revealed my ample cleavage, "Come on in, I'm so hot for y…."

Leah stood outside the door, holding Jordan's hand. She smirked, "I hope you don't mind, but this little boy isn't feeling very well."

"Of course, sorry, it was the lunch," I stammered unconvincingly, clutching my stomach. I moved out of the way.

Walking down the aisle, I could see Ben sniggering behind his paper. I elbowed him in the head as I returned to my seat.

"Where were you?" I asked between clenched teeth.

"About a minute after you left that kid started muttering about feeling ill."

Those parents are positively neglectful, I thought, giving them dirty looks. The mother was happily sipping a glass of wine while the father was enjoying a nap. I had a good mind to report them to Social Services.

I was distracted, though, by the rattle of the trolley once again as Oliver brought round the duty-free goods. "I could do with

123

some new perfume," I said, smiling at Ben sweetly. He owed me after the toilet fiasco.

"Go on, then."

Jordan returned, still green in the face. I rested back against my seat and closed my eyes, trying to conjure up images of shimmering seas and silky soft sand between my toes, Ben's urgent kisses on my neck. I filtered out Jordan and Connor's whining voices as they started thumping each other viciously on the legs, catching me occasionally with their sharp fists.

I must have drifted off, as I was woken by the smooth, insincere tones of the captain. "Thank you for travelling with Redman's Airline. It is now four o'clock local time. The crew and I would like to wish you a very enjoyable holiday and we hope to see you again soon."

"Wake up, droopy drawers," Ben said, nudging me. "We're here. You've been talking in your sleep and making some really strange noises. You put on quite a show for the other passengers. You'll have to tell me what you were dreaming about."

I wiped the dried saliva from my chin and gave Ben a wobbly smile.

"Sunny Malaga, here we come," he said, rising up and reaching for his rucksack in the compartment above.

"Can you get mine, too?" Jordan said.

"No problem, mate." Ben grabbed the other bag and as he lifted it a bright orange liquid gushed over his head and down his shirt.

"My Lucozade!" Jordan yelped.

"Don't worry, Ben," I said with a smirk, raising the window blind, "the rain will wash it off."

Untitled

Ansley Moon

These days
words
are foreigners
to me.
They speak
nothing
that I understand.
To them
I am a stranger.
A distant memory,
an ex-lover.
Too current
to forget.
And too painful
to remember.

A Field of Cornflowers

Caroline Hawkes

Two swans groomed themselves in the rain. Large white feathers were plucked out of glossy wings and tossed away to get caught in the churning, eddying swirl of dirty rainwater surging down the road. The feathers bobbed along hopefully, like the white flags on surrendering ships, before being sucked into the drains.

The rain drummed at the doors and windows, while the oak tree scraped its knotted branches across the roof. Having failed to make an impression on the day, the sun retired behind the far hills. Inside the house, Constantine pressed her palm against her chest. The rat-tat-tat of droplets on glass resonated with the pumping of her heart and she feared that at any moment it might shatter.

She moved aside the window drape. The sun was pulling the colour and light out of the sky. Dragged down behind it, the darkness descended in several shades, spreading across the clouds like ink on blotting paper. Through the blue-grey gloom

Constantine could see the rising waters whirling around the gatepost. She let the curtain fall back into place and sat down beside the fire.

Two days ago she had folded together three sheets of thin cream paper before wrapping them in a piece of grey felt. She had covered her head and shoulders with a heavy blanket and left the house. Keeping close to the wall, she hurried down the lane until she reached the crossroads. After checking that there was nobody else around, she scrambled over the wall and into the field beyond. For several seconds she remained where she had landed, her back against the mossy stone, her breath catching the back of her throat.

Under the scrutiny of a kestrel, its brick-red back turned to the sky, Constantine began to run her hands over the wall. When she found what she was looking for she pushed her fingers between the stones and eased out a large flint-dappled rock, allowing just enough room to let her hand pass. Inside she located a bundle of fabric. She replaced it with her own and moved the block back into place, filling the gaps around it with the displaced earth.

*   *   *

For two nights Constantine had waited and yesterday the rain had begun. As she was kneeling by the hearth, laying kindling over dried grasses, she had heard the first few drops pinging against the inside of the chimneybreast. Once the fire had taken hold she had dragged sandbags across the bottoms of the doors and prayed that he would soon arrive.

*   *   *

127

But now, sitting by the fire, Constantine reached into her pocket and brought out the parcel of fabric. She pressed it against her nose; it smelled old and musty, like the damp soil brushed off ancient tombs. Inside was a small piece of rolled up paper and a silver cross. With her dirtied fingers she unfurled the paper. Written, in a light, looping hand, were the words Tomorrow. I will be with you tomorrow. The noise of a song thrush, beating the shell of a snail against the window ledge, disturbed her and she pressed the cross to her forehead before wrapping it back up and returning it to her pocket.

For a moment she placed her small hands over her face before brushing back her pale hair. She had barely eaten in days and the hunger was carving hollows in her cheeks and darkening the circles under her green eyes. If he didn't arrive by sunrise she would have to leave alone.

Twilight was rubbing the hard edges off the corners of the room. Constantine took a candle down into the kitchen and broke the last chair into pieces with a hatchet. She emptied a pail of water that had been collecting from a drip in the ceiling, where the wind had slipped its fingers between the roof slates and picked them off. Every movement was slow and deliberate. She stacked the pieces of broken chair next to the fire and brought the blanket around her.

*   *   *

Constantine slept fitfully. In her dreams the house was filled with people and suffused with a warm yellow light. All the doors and windows were opened wide and the sound of bird chatter was carried into the house on a gentle breeze. The oak tree outside was

128

covered in thick glossy leaves and appeared to be sitting back in satisfaction.

Everyone was wearing clothes made of brightly coloured fabric, some stitched or finished with gold threading or cord. Plump arms waved in the air and cheeks swelled with laughter. A small butterfly with delicate lilac wings fluttered in through the window and weaved through the assembly. Time slowed as Constantine watched the butterfly. As it danced in a beam of sunshine she heard every flap of its wings as a slow muffled heartbeat and followed the trail of fine silvery dust left in its wake.

In the corner of the room a child was turning the handle of an oversized gramophone. The noises got louder and the colour began to drain out of the clothes. The laughter began to warp and curdle in the air, and the merry faces distort. Constantine realised that she didn't recognise any of the people and their presence became more and more threatening. She felt as though she was shrinking. The faces leered down at her like crumbling limestone gargoyles squatting underneath the arches of a gothic church.

Constantine woke up shivering. The last few embers crackled softly in the grate and she piled on the last of the wood, closing the top of the burner and opening up the bottom to encourage it to draw. She curled back up and rested her head on the inside of her arm. Slipping her right hand into her pocket, she wrapped her fingers around the cloth parcel. The drip in the kitchen seemed louder and the rain outside, heavier.

*   *   *

She imagined Sebastian lifting her up and whispering into her ear.

129

He carried her through choppy brown water and put her down into a small, round boat that made her think of a walnut shell. Her arm dangled over the side of the boat and the force of the current dragged it behind them, fine green weeds entwining her fingers. A thin sliver of the sun could be seen emerging from a clump of trees in the east. A pair of swans paddled past the boat.

*   *   *

When Constantine was eight years old her mother woke her one morning at dawn, pressed her finger to her lips and helped her into her clothes. She had packed some of their belongings into a large canvas sack and, without saying a word to anybody, they left their home. They climbed into the back of a pale-blue truck and spent several hours bumping through unfamiliar countryside. Her mother watched the road disappear behind them with glistening eyes while Constantine peered through the cracks in the bottom of the truck and watched the brown stone earth blur beneath them. An elderly man, with a gap between his front teeth, sat opposite Constantine. He was wearing dusty corduroy trousers that had a hole in each knee. He made her shudder and press herself closer to her mother's side.

When the truck stopped, the driver got out and came around to the back to help Constantine's mother get down. They spoke to each other in quiet, urgent voices while the man held on to her forearms and shook them gently. Constantine didn't remember having ever seen him before, this friend of her mother's. She was afraid that they would leave her with the gap-toothed man, so she climbed down onto the road, dragging their bag behind her. Before the driver returned to the vehicle, Constantine's mother reached

130

underneath the collar of her coat and pulled out the thin red scarf that had been tied around her neck. She put it into the man's hand, caught a hold of Constantine and turned her back. The van left with a screech, the wheels churning up the earth, puffing out a cloud of dust. A flock of starlings rose up from the reed beds on one side of the road and scattered across the sky above them like a crocheted blanket. Constantine turned around to watch the truck leave. The gap-toothed man held up his hand in a solemn wave.

Constantine never forgot how tired her legs felt and how warm and dry her mother's hand was as they walked to the bridge. Occasionally they stopped and sat down beside the road and her mother would give her biscuits to eat and water to drink. But mostly they just walked, hand in hand, Constantine trailing behind her mother.

Long after the sun had set, and as the brushed charcoal sky threatened rain, they reached the border. They hid themselves amongst densely packed ash trees and waited until the patrol had moved on. When Constantine's mother could no longer see the sweep of headlights, they crept out from their cover. She'd been told that when it passed she would have twenty minutes to get herself and her child safely to the other side.

*　　*　　*

They made their home in a cottage on the outskirts of a village. It was rented from a local landowner on the condition that they kept themselves to themselves. He was more interested in money than popularity with the villagers, but he didn't want to push it too far. Her mother made handicrafts that she sold in the markets in nearby

131

towns and Constantine sometimes ran errands for the local women.

One spring it rained for weeks on end and no one came to the markets to buy her mother's goods. On the day that Randall, their landlord, came around to collect the rent, Constantine was sent out. She knew that they did not have enough money to pay it and that her mother was planning to negotiate more time.

When Constantine had grown bored of running through the long grass in the fields near her home, when she was fed up of laying on her back counting the birds that flew over her head, and when she felt sick from all the nectar she had sucked out of the wild honeysuckle, she returned home. Just as she reached the gate of their cottage, Randall appeared on the other side. He was tucking the tails of his shirt into his trousers. He flung open the gate and bristled past without meeting her eye.

The back door was ajar and Constantine slipped noise-lessly into the kitchen. A chair had been knocked over and was lying in the centre of the room. Her mother was sitting on the stone steps that led to the living room. Her knees were drawn up in front of her and her face buried in her arms. She was wearing a long maroon-coloured skirt, which Constantine noticed had been torn at the hem. Feeling a presence in the room, her mother looked up. As soon as she saw her daughter she got up, straightened her clothes and wiped her hands over her face.

From then on they saw little of Randall and the next time the rent was due he sent his son. Constantine didn't know that he even had a son. She blushed when she opened the front door. He was quick to smile and when he spoke, his words were carefully considered. Flustered, she invited him in for a moment while she fetched the rent. As Sebastian took the money, his fingertips gently brushed the underside of her hand.

*   *   *

For months before her mother died Constantine nursed her through several illnesses. On the days when she felt up to it, she taught Constantine weaving or wood carving, so she could take her place at the market. But Constantine was afraid to leave her mother for too long and always came back from the market without selling much. Her mother would tell her off for not bringing home enough money, but the relief on her face was visible and reassured Constantine that she had done the right thing.

Sebastian came to collect the rent and Constantine would give him all she could, but it was never enough. He would tell her that he'd managed to persuade his father to give them a bit of leeway, considering that they had been such good tenants for all these years and that her mother was so gravely ill. The truth was that Sebastian dare not even broach the subject of the rent with his father and for some time had supplemented it himself. When he could carry on no longer he mustered up his courage and spoke to his father. Randall, in an accommodating mood, agreed to give Constantine more time.

On the day after the death of her mother, Randall paid Constantine a visit. He would be returning in a week to collect the money that he was owed. When he left, Constantine sat down on the kitchen steps and wept. She wasn't sure how much she owed, but she knew that she couldn't possibly pay it. Constantine remembered vividly what happened to her mother the last time they failed to pay. She remembered standing at the kitchen door and how, after she had wiped her face and straightened her clothes, her mother had limped across the room to hold Constantine to her bosom. The only time that Constantine had ever heard her mother sob, even throughout her illnesses, was that night – that night after Randall had visited to collect money they didn't have. The sound of her mother crying had seeped through the bedroom wall and terrified her.

*   *   *

Sebastian reached across and fished her arm out of the water. He patted it dry and tucked it underneath the blanket. It had been more difficult than he had thought to steal his father's boat. The rain had kept him at home, so he hadn't been able to leave when he'd planned. If his father found out that he'd been courting Constantine he would almost certainly be disowned. He was worried that Constantine may have thought that he had changed his mind and had stopped waiting for him. He dreaded reaching the cottage and finding it empty.

*   *   *

Constantine could see grey-brown figures flickering between the trees. She could hear footsteps falling with soft thuds onto a carpet of dried leaves. The noise of quickening breath mingled with the sighing of the woods. When Constantine stopped, turned her head and squinted her eyes, all movements seemed to cease. When they reached the bridge, Constantine wrapped her hands around the wooden railings. Her mother leaned in close to her ear and whispered encouragement. The bridge was narrow and only allowed them to cross in single file. The planks underneath Constantine's feet felt loose and rickety and she was scared that she might lose her footing and slip between them, into the gorge below. Her mother nudged her forward.

The sound of her own breathing filled her ears and the terror of the unknown clutched at her heart. When she got to the middle of the bridge, halfway between the past and the future, she stopped. In the distance an owl screeched and she couldn't be sure if it came from behind them or in front. Again she felt her mother close behind her lean in and whisper in her ear. Years later, the only word that she could remember was 'promise.'

*　　*　　*

Constantine was lying in the bottom of the boat. A rolled- up blanket cushioned her head and her breath rose and fell quietly. Sunlight bathed her face and warmed her eyelids. They were approaching a small wooden jetty and Sebastian began to steer them towards it. He pulled the boat up close, looping the rope around a post. For a few moments more he watched Constantine sleep and then leaned across and kissed her softly on the side of her head, where her hair curled and feathered. Sebastian then stepped gently out of the boat before unhooking the rope and pushing it back out into the river.

Constantine sighed. The boat rocked slightly as it changed its course. After a few moments she opened her eyes. Above her the sky stretched out wide like a field of cornflowers. She felt as though the trees behind her gathered together, extending their boughs to push her forward, and the willows that lined the riverbanks seemed to wave her on with their long, spindly branches. A kingfisher flashed turquoise in front of her and a pair of dragonflies hovered nearby. Constantine sat up in the boat and smiled.

Lycanthropy

Bethany Pope

He grips the butt between his teeth and tastes the gritty remains of wet tobacco on his tongue. The sun slants down and slashes into his unprotected eyes, and he moves his tattered hat forward so that the brim provides some cover. Dried salt from dried sweat collects and stings against his skin, abrading and firing it with a chemical burn. His horse dropped dead days ago, crumbling into sand and bone. He has walked in a reasonably straight line since then, worn boots sinking into piled sand, following the rise and fall of the steady sun and the inconstant moon.

The polished cedar gun-handles at his side glimmer and shine in the descending light. They catch and hold the dying sun and are trapped, reflected, in his eyes. He has not looked toward the horizon since his horse took its last stumbling step and collapsed into the ground, spraying the sand with the precious lather from its sides.

He spits out the butt, grimacing at the wasted saliva coating the end, and reaches a gnarled but well-learned hand into his poke for more tobacco and a paper to roll. The smoking gives him something to think about other than the unending heat, the dead behind him, and the death in front. His fingers are clumsy from exhaustion and his tobacco low from days of travel. In time, he gets one rolled and lights up with a sulphur match, taken from a dwindling supply. The flame catches and reflects the dying rays of the setting sun. He breathes in and the ash grows long and whitish grey. He exhales and the smoke curls up toward the sky like an offering for the gods. It disperses and turns aside.

He can recall the last bed he knew. He can feel her fingers curled through his hair, gently pulling like a fine comb. He can remember the strength of her thighs, the solid roundness of her rump and the weight of her curled against him in the dark on those yellowed, dirty sheets. Water was precious, and dirt could be beaten out. They drank whisky before and after, rolling their tongues over the char-wood taste of the liquor and the sour flavour of themselves.

He can remember the smell of the hairs at the nape of her neck. She smelled like violet water, superficially, a thin patina of floral scent above the stronger cat-smell of her sex. Thick black hairs merged into unwashed, greyish skin, pale just where the twain did meet. In the dark he breathed her in like smoke; he drank her waters under the cover of the changing moon.

*   *   *

The night before he bought his horse she called out sharply and clawed him deep across his back. He growled, way back down in his throat, and nipped her gently with his teeth. She, roused from

137

her nightmare, kicked out violently and tumbled out of bed with a thump. She looked, surprised, through the window at the waxing moon.

It stood out, yellow and full as a woman's breast, high in the sky unobscured by clouds. Her hair fell in a rope down her back, and the rope held the moonlight. He sat up, naked as his day of birth, save for the thatch of hair, which clothes all men, and reached out toward her to pull her up.

She lay still in the dust, tied by the moon, and gazed uncomprehending at his fingers as they uncurled in invitation. Biting her lip, she gave him her hand. The moonlight caught on his teeth as he smiled.

"Whose name did you call?"

"It was a dream."

His fingers tightened across her wrist; his long sharp nails drew a drop of blood.

"Whose name did you call?"

His voice was cold and solid, without a tremble and without the warmth of anger or fear. Her voice shook and her gaze was blue and open.

"It was a dream."

*   *   *

He left her body cold and empty, covered in blood and the chill of the moon. He could still taste her in the morning, strong against his teeth. He did not think about her eyes, or the fall of her hair, or the gentle pressure of her fingers, or the nimble workings of her small pink tongue. He closed and locked the door.

He bought the horse with a minimum of haggling – just enough to avoid suspicion, not enough to be memorable – and set out to face the setting sun. He has travelled days in the afternoon heat and in the bitter cold of the desert night. He has built his fires from tumbleweed and gorse, eaten the natural jerky by the sides of the road, when there was a road, and scattered around the rocks when there was not. He has drunk his own sweat and the sweat of the horse.

He has caught a scent, off in the distance. He finishes the cigarette and puts his nose down to the trail. He heads off into the rising sun.

The Break of a New Day

Kelly Fitzgerald

Mike Smith has a hard time calling himself an artist. He is still a student, after all, earning his art degree; or maybe it's because he's tried a few jobs and not found his niche; or it could be because he's dabbled in many forms of artistry, but not declared a favorite medium.

Yet times are a-changin' for Smith, who might call himself an artist after all.

"I always considered it a grandiose label to stick on me, but I suppose it's that or nothing," Smith says. And the M.A. Creative Writing students at Trinity College, Carmarthen are thrilled he went with just that. Otherwise, they might not have his artwork, *Frozen Morning*, for their *De/tached* book cover.

Smith is what you'd call an untraditional or mature student. He's a 51-year-old Neath, Wales, native that is back in school. Attending Swansea Institute of Higher Education for his

140

undergraduate degree in Fine Arts & Combined Media, Smith is currently in his second of four years, attending part-time.

The degree involves a variety of media, including film, ceramics, and painting – really everything – and that suits Smith just fine. "I use whatever I consider appropriate for the meaning I wish to convey," he says. "I'm in the company of many other artists, which has allowed me to become more experimental." He's also made a new batch of friends.

But Smith's road to Swansea Institute wasn't that direct.

Smith tried working as a civil servant with the Driver and Vehicle Licensing Agency (DVLA), but adds that he was "at the wrong place at the wrong time," finding more fulfillment in constructing mobiles out of drawing pins, than the actual work. Smith also tried his hand – a bit more successfully – at graphic design, working in the industry for five years, in London.

But eventually, Smith found his way back to art, something he had sidetracked from after painting when he was young and winning a few competitions in junior school. Things seem to fit much better. Monumental in this life-change was Smith discovering art as an aid to what had been plaguing him for years: alcoholism.

"I was lucky in my timing regarding going back to University. I started two weeks after giving up alcohol, having been a full-blown alcoholic for the best part of ten very unproductive years," Smith says. "Without exaggeration, I can say it was University and giving up the drink which means I am here now. I was that close to the end."

As a result, Smith is at a new beginning, something Trinity students and other admirers of his work are now able to witness;

it's a sober start filled with imaginative art, like the piece *Frozen Morning*.

Frozen Morning came from an assignment set at Swansea Institute. The task was a photo-realism painting and the result was a multi-layered, multi-medium piece that began with Smith simply taking a picture of himself on the street in Neath. "It's just the road I walk every day. That's all really."

Of course, *Frozen Morning* is much more than that. The photograph is digitally enhanced, and Smith added texture to the piece using a variety of acrylics, enamel paint and fountain pens of varying thicknesses. A scouring knife and intentional cigarette burns were also parts of the process.

When working on the piece, Smith's girlfriend, Elizabeth Bates, commented that she couldn't paint to save her life. So, in order to prove her wrong, Smith recruited her to draw part of the pavement in the bottom section of the piece. Expert eyes may decipher some of their alternative title, which is scratched in. Smith recalls it going something like, "My girlfriend told me that she couldn't do a photo-realist painting to save her life, but I gave her this part of the painting to do and this is the result." Of course, Smith didn't end up going with that title. The final name of the piece, *Frozen Morning*, has less of a story, and simply came to Smith late at night.

Frozen Morning was discovered by a few of Trinity's M.A. students when they were scouring Carmarthen galleries for talent. Their final stop was the King Street Gallery, and Smith's piece happened to be hanging on the wall – he had submitted the piece for the gallery's art contest after seeing an advert posted at his University.

Smith can't help but add, "I didn't win, by the way," although

Trinity's creative writing students would beg to differ. The piece that took about two weeks to make, created in his bedroom, and that Smith thought he'd never actually finish, is now Trinity's anthology cover. They chose the piece for its mysterious, 'unexpected visitor' aura, which lends itself perfectly to the book's relationships theme.

After revelling in his newfound praise, what's next for artist Mike Smith? Finishing his degree of course, while hopefully following in the footsteps of his favored artists, like Marcel Duchamp. He's also submitting his artwork to as many exhibitions as he can, hoping to sell such pieces as *Frozen Morning*.

"I wonder whether I chose art or if it was forced on me," Smith says, "being the only thing it seemed I could do well." Perhaps time – or a few *De/tached* sales – will reveal the answer.

NOTES ON THE AUTHORS

Ansley Moon
Born in New Delhi, India and raised in the United States, Ansley Moon calls Atlanta, Georgia home. After abandoning dolls and Barbies, she started writing and has been doing so for sixteen years. She received her B.A. in English, with a minor in History, from Georgia State University, and spent one year of her undergraduate degree at Northumbria University in Newcastle, England. Since her student loans were not high enough, she decided to get an M.A. in Creative Writing. Once she completes her Master's degree she plans to return to the United States.

Bethany Pope
Bethany Pope is a twenty-two-year-old girl from Texas who collects comic books, writes a lot of mostly unpublishable poems and short stories, and still lives with her parents. Technically. She is currently parking her things in a room the size of a thimble and is happier for it. Since coming to Wales she has discovered the beauty of the landscape, the majesty of the seaside, and the joy of curry. She also enjoys throwing things at sheep, but only when there is no one around.

Caroline Hawkes
Caroline Hawkes likes the short story for its ability to say so much in so few words – for what is not said, alongside what is. She agrees with Raymond Carver, who says that in a short story it is "possible to write about commonplace things and endow those things with immense, even startling, power." Caroline lives in Pembrokeshire and works in education.

David Jones

Born, educated and based in the Carmarthen area for most of his life, he retired from a thirty-seven-year career in the National Health Service in 2003. His serious creative writing interests were conceived with his song-writing exploits as a member of several bilingual local bands from the 70's onward. A number of his poems have been published through such vehicles as Forward Press and Anchor Books. His main literary interests include scriptwriting, songs and poetry. Currently, he is embarking on a biographical account of Welsh Rugby International players who have emerged from Carmarthen Athletic RFC. Outside of that he runs a small business in collectable memorabilia, mainly vinyl records and rugby programmes.

Dian Jenkins

Born and bred in Cardigan, Ceredigion, I taught for thirty-five years and now find myself returning to Trinity College where I qualified in Music and the teaching of four- to seven-year-olds in the 60's. As a bilingual writer, I've always enjoyed the rhythm of music and words and since my early retirement through deafness, have found an outlet in writing and composing songs for children. In 2002, I composed a collection of songs, *Anifeiliaid Anwes* (pets), with Fflach studios in Cardigan, followed by *Rhifo* (counting) the following year. In 2005, I launched a CD of songs suitable for seven- to nine-year-olds to complement my daughter's series of books called *Siani'r Shetland*.

Jacqui Burns

Jacqui Burns juggles with so many balls that most of them end up on the floor. As well as bringing up her daughter alone, she teaches full-time at a secondary school and is studying for her M.A. in

Creative Writing. Inevitably, some things are neglected, usually a neat house, diet and exercise! Jacqui has written many short stories, none of which have been serious and edifying. The comic aspects of life appeal to her: "All over Britain there are cracked pavements ready to trip me up and drunks waiting to sit by me on the bus." She is currently writing her first novel and is poised to suck up to any publishers willing to give her a deal.

Judith Barrow

Judith Barrow has had various short stories, poems, plays, reviews and articles published throughout the British Isles. She has won poetry competitions, including the 2004 Roundyhouse Annual competition and the Landsker prize for humourous poetry and particularly enjoys writing performance poetry. Judith has a B.A. (Hons.) in Literature and has studied drama and script writing. She has had two plays performed in the 'Play Off' competition at the Dylan Thomas Centre in Swansea. Born in Lancashire and brought up in a small village near the Pennines, she moved to Pembrokeshire in 1978. She is a founding member of the Tenby Writers' Circle. Judith has submitted a children's novel to publishers, and has recently completed an anthology of short stories for children. Currently, she is working on a saga set during the Second World War.

Kelly Fitzgerald

Raised on the banks of Minnesota's Centerville Lake, Kelly has traveled far in her twenty-four years: she earned a B.A. in Journalism and Mass Communications from Creighton University in Nebraska, fulfilled her electives at the National University of Ireland, Galway and now completes her Masters in Creative

Writing from Trinity College, Carmarthen in Wales. Yet she will always return home to the Land of Ten Thousand Lakes, where she first grasped her love for writing (Visitation High School), where she earned her first regular writing wage (Greenspring Media Group), and where her parents, twin sister and three brothers call home. Whether non-fiction or true to her imagination, Kelly has traveled far and has many more stories to tell.

Nadine Fry

I've lived in Carmarthenshire my whole life until December of last year when my husband and I, along with our four-year-old son and two cats, emigrated to Canada. I was already halfway through my Creative Writing M.A. at Trinity, so, after some juggling around, we worked out a way that I could continue the course via e-mail, airmail and help from some good friends. I have been writing for quite a few years now, including mainly short stories for both adults and children. My dream is to be a published children's author and to visit the Welsh ocean as often as possible.

Nicky Herriot

Having spent her childhood living in various countries, Nicky Herriot has lived in Wales all her adult life and attempts to pay the bills by working on county council road safety projects. She took up writing seriously five years ago and is serving her apprenticeship by being rejected by some of the best publishers in Britain. Nicky is relieved by the fact that her family is not too dysfunctional, as she can only write when she is happy and stress-free. Her one claim to fame is that she has had two of her short stories printed in the national magazine *DIVA*. Sadly, in one of them, the last paragraph, with the punchline, was missed out.

Sandra Mackness

Sandra was born one stormy night in South Wales where she remained until absconding to become a Butlin Redcoat. Employment in aviation and hotels often led to surreal experiences, as did the years of running a Wiltshire guesthouse with her late husband. Since moving back to Wales, she has worked in Child Protection as a minute-taker. A move to Ammanford coincided with the start of her M.A. course and her introduction to the Peacock Vein ScriptShop, along with a writing group called Hookers' Pen. 2005 saw several of her short stories in print; also an ambition fulfilled when she ran her own creative writing workshops. Sandra kicked off 2006 with publication of a short story in a *Black Lace* anthology. She hopes to spend as much time as possible writing and travelling.

Sharon Tregenza

Sharon Tregenza has had over 300 short stories, articles and poems published and broadcast worldwide. She's also won several competitions in poetry and fiction – some of her odder successes include a £500 first prize in a 'local limerick' competition judged by Ronnie Corbett and read out on the *Two Ronnies*, as well as having a humour poem, submitted to the American publication, *The Saturday Evening Post*, published in the column of the evangelist Billy Graham. Born and raised in Penzance, Cornwall, Sharon is intensely proud of her Cornish heritage. She lived in Cyprus and the Middle East for many years before moving to the Pembrokeshire border less than a year ago. Now, concentrating on writing for children, she has four picture books being submitted to publishers and is working on her second novel.

Sue Moss

It is a truth universally acknowledged that teaching full-time for almost twenty years will lead a person to seriously question if she is making the most of her life. Should the answer to the question be in the negative, it is best advised for said person to get off her backside and change things. So, if that's one route to happiness the other is surely to buy a house with excellent transport links to an international airport, which specialises in offering cheap flights to Paris on a daily basis.

Trinity's M.A. Creative Writing students would particularly like to acknowledge:

Trinity College, Carmarthen, for its support and funding.

Course Directors Paul Wright and Menna Elfyn, for their leadership.

Mike Smith, for his stunning cover art *Frozen Morning*.

Kitty Sewell and Phil Carradice for their time and energy.

Menter A Business, for its financial aid and business advice.

The Parthian staff, for their help and guidance.

And lastly, our families, for their unending encouragement.

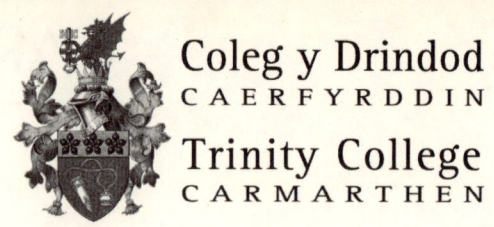

Coleg y Drindod
CAERFYRDDIN
Trinity College
CARMARTHEN

MA in Creative Writing

Trinity's MA in Creative Writing is designed for committed writers who wish to complete significant pieces of work and generally broadened their experience as writers.

The workshop programme is run by one of Wales' leading writers, Menna Elfyn. It draws upon a number of adjunct writing staff, and the support of academics experienced in the teaching of all aspects of creative writing.

In addition to the course itself the College supports a number of reading and social events in which you would be able to participate, as well as the publication of a course anthology showcasing students' work.

Study can either be full-time over one year, or part-time over two.

For further information, contact:
Dr Paul Wright
School of Creative Arts and Humanites
Tel: 01267 676721
Email: p.wright@trinity-cm.ac.uk
or the Faculty Office 01267 676696
Trinity College Carmarthen
Wales, SA31 3EP